FROM THE LIBRARY OF

helen a. beilinson

**S** T O R I E   S

schemes

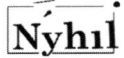

*Vera & Linus*

Copyright © 2006 by Jesse Ball and Thordis Björnsdottir

All rights reserved. No part of this book may be used or reproduced in any manner whatsoever without written permission except in the case of brief quotations embodied in critical articles and reviews. Printed in Iceland by ODDI. Inquiries regarding this book should be directed to Nyhil, Laugavegur 59, IS-101 Reykjavik, Iceland.

**FIRST EDITION**

ISBN: 9979-9715-6-8
ISBN: 978-9979-9715-6-6

**T e x t :** Th., J.B.
**Translation:** Th., J.B.
**Design, Layout:** J. B.
**Drawings:** J. B.
**Frontispiece still:** Catherine Despont
**Image Suiting:** William Rahilly

Grateful Acknowledgement to CONDUIT, in whose pages "the Method for Waylayers" first appeared.

0.3.1

For six who know well what we say:

# THE DISAS-
# TROUS TALE OF
# VERA & LINUS

0.5.1

ORDER [a number . a number . a number] The FIRST: 1 means Thordis Björnsdóttir; 2 means Jesse Ball. The SECOND designates the story's position. The THIRD lists sections, sometimes displaced.

?.?.?

0.8.1

But when Archimedes began to ply his engines, he at once shot against the land forces all sorts of missile weapons, and immense masses of stone that came down with incredible noise and violence; against which no man could stand; for they knocked down those upon whom they fell in heaps, breaking all their ranks and files. In the meantime huge poles thrust out from the walls over the ships sunk some by the great weights, which they let down from on high upon them; others they lifted up into the air by an iron hand or beak like a crane's beak and, when they had drawn them up by the prow, and set them on end upon the poop, they plunged them to the bottom of the sea; or else the ships, drawn by engines within, and whirled about, were dashed against steep rocks that stood jutting out under the walls, with great destruction of the soldiers that were aboard them. A ship was frequently lifted up to a great height in the air (a dreadful thing to behold), and was rolled to and fro, and kept swinging, until the mariners were all thrown out, when at length it was dashed against the rocks, or let fall.

Plutarch, *Life of Marcellus* (tr. John Dryden)

# V

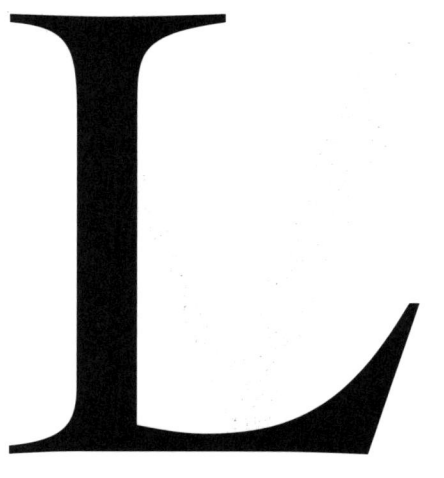

Vera and Linus went to bury the book up hill and down across unkempt grass through a close wood to a dry lake. There was water there, but it was dry.

—You first, said Vera.

Linus lowered his head. In he went.

At the bottom of the lake
was an underground stream.

They took it awhile like a road

and soon came to a clearing in a buried forest.

As if alighting from a horse, they climbed down.

From her coat, Vera drew a trowel.

—This will do nicely, said Linus.

And they stood together over late winter grasses
where curled flowers without color bent like limbs.

Linus went to the chest in the room at the back of the house, the chest he had kept closed since 6 May. He unlocked it with a little iron key, saying,

—Key, I have kept you on a string about my neck these many years. Serve me now.

The chest opened.

Inside was a girl, bound and gagged. She began to wriggle violently. Her eyes blinked and blinked in the sudden light.

—Vera! called Linus.

Vera came in from the next room wearing her dust-clothes as though recently come from a motorcar.

—Here is your present, he said.

Vera looked in the chest. A smile ran along her hand out onto Linus's shoulder.

—What will we do with her? she asked.

Linus reached down and caught the tied up girl by the throat.

—That's not all, he said. There're two more beneath!

He yanked the first up out of the box and threw her onto the ground by her neck. Sure enough, there were two others underneath.

—How grand!

Vera gave a little cry and did a jump in the air.

—Can I name them? she asked.

—They have names already, said Linus, but we can remove them if we want. And why shouldn't we?

He yanked out the two remaining girls and threw them beside the first. All were furiously blinking and wriggling.

Beneath the girls there was a lake and a sailboat.

—Shall we? asked Linus, for the sun was shining and a proper breeze had just begun.

—But won't they escape? asked Vera.

—I shouldn't think so, said Linus, but to be sure …

He gave Vera a knife, and she cut an ankle off of each. Then they went sailing.

Linus had made a dress for Vera. The dress was of
dark green material with two pockets
attached by a thick and brown string of leather.

They had sewn one of the pockets together but inside
five little children were in a silent heap.

The other pocket was open. It was slightly smaller;
inside there was a single child behaving badly, repeatedly sticking its head up.

—I want to go home, it whined.

—Never! Vera said and pushed the head down.

Crying then inside the pocket and striving around.

—We must sew this one up as well, said Linus.
Otherwise we get no peace.

—I agree with you, said Vera.

Linus sought a thread and a needle and started slowly
sewing the pocket together. The child's crying
increased and it tried to squeeze both hands and head
through the hole. But Vera pushed it back down and
all the while Linus kept on with the sewing.

Vera felt the child kicking and struggling in the pocket.
But the wailing soon became less, at last turning to
quiet sobbing. Then Linus finished the sewing.

Day passed, and the child's movements kept on. Now
and then one could hear it sobbing in the pocket.

By evening the child had stopped struggling.
No sound came from it any more, neither wailing nor sobbing. No sound anymore.

Vera decided to hide from Linus. She crawled under the bed and waited there. She did not have to wait long.

A moment and a moment and then Linus was walking about the place where she was hidden, calling out:

—Vera my Vera! Where are you?

Finally he opened the front door and shouted her name into the street. But at the same moment he heard a voice whispering in his ear:

—Vera is here no longer. I saw her sneaking out before and now she is gone.

Linus was awfully startled; he rushed out of the house. He turned around and around and then started running faster and faster in the hopes of finding his Vera.

She herself knew nothing of what had happened. She herself still waited for Linus to find her,
still waited in her hiding place under the bed.

In the night, Vera cut off all of Linus's hair. She put the hair in a glass tube.

and when he woke, she threatened him with it
and all day
until his hair grew back

he had to do exactly what she said.

—I'll break it with a hammer, said Vera. I goddamn will.

Vera waited inside the room with the victim tied by hand and foot.

She knew that Linus would soon be there with the knife in his pocket, or that is what she thought.

And for the whole night she waited and waited, believing her Linus would bring the knife.

Linus was sleeping. Vera wanted to wake him. She was lonely and it was very dark all through the house and all through the town. Someone had been murdered and stuffed into a tree and so it was dark, as always, when such things happen.

—What will I do? asked Vera.

She took out her little Russian doll.

—Which of you is smartest? she asked, looking at them all lined up.

—Ask advice of me, said one.

—I'm the most well-traveled, said another.

—What a lie, said a third. You've never left this room.

And it was true. She had been made in that very room by an old Russian man many years before, when he had stopped for the night in that humble town.

—What must I do? asked Vera.

—Jump off the roof, said one, and you will join him in his dream.

—A lie, said another, a malicious lie.

—Stern truth, said a third, and timely at that.

Up then, Vera, to the roof. And off.

# The Willow Path

A man in town knew about Vera and Linus, yet still he asked Vera if she would go walking with him, still he spoke to her as if he would like to be her lover.

—Go with him then, said Linus, and expect me by the willow tree that stands so proudly by the riverside.

So Vera went into town and took this town-man walking to the river. She did not suffer him to touch her, and she did not speak to him kindly. Yet still she led him down the path.

In the stable, Linus gathered himself. He put on his hate-coat of black stiffness, and his gloves of madness, and upon his feet his iron-shod boots.

—Watch how I go, he said to his dark preparations.

Then through the wood by a hidden way, the willow path, they called it ever after, in tribute to the thing he would then do.

Behind the willow, Linus. Up the river road, Vera and the town-man.

—It is nice here by the river, said Vera. One can hear the hours stirring in their sleep.

—Is it that, said the town-man, or just the world trembling at the touch of your beauty?

Out then Linus from behind the willow. He held a

black hate in his hands, a red hate in his eyes, and a yellow hate laced like light through his boots.

—I am for you, he said,

and he took the town-man's neck and broke it with the strength of his hands.

—Sleep, said Linus. Sleep awhile.

And he tossed the limp body into the water.

—Shall we dance? asked Vera, lifting up her dress to show her ankles.

—Let us dance, said Linus.

And then they were three dancing, three then four then five — Vera, Linus, the willow path, the moon, and again the willow path.

They all stood silently in a line beside the wall, shivering with fear.

Vera came up to each one whispering several words in the ear. Then she went to Linus.

—And now we shall start, she said with a grin.

Vera and Linus took a child from a window where it was sitting.

—Has anyone punished you in this recent while? asked Vera.

—No, said the child, for I am very good and always do what I am told.

—Well, that, said Linus, will not save you now.

Then they took this child of goodness and gave it something nice to eat and something nice to drink and played with it and sang to it and then they buried it alive in the thin grass so that only its hand stuck out of the earth and they watched the hand as it clutched and clutched at nothing until finally it seized it and was gone.

—Let us go, said Vera to Linus, to picnic with the buried child.

So they packed a lovely picnic basket, you know Vera is awfully good at putting together a fine basket with wine from the south and delicious sharp hard cheese from the mountains, with fruit from the beloved orchards of Montlatl, and nuts from the fields of Rút. Secretly also, Vera packed the darkest chocolate as a surprise.

—Carry this, you, said Vera, handing the basket to Linus.

She took up the blanket and also a length of rope and a knife with which to make a trap.

Vera and Linus found a large and long box made from wood.

—Here I want to go, said Vera and lay down in the box.

She fit herself perfectly in, then smiled and closed her eyes.

—I will go then, Linus said and started walking away.

But when he had taken several steps he realized that he was incapable of leaving Vera behind in the box. He walked back and had a look in. But Vera was no longer there. The box was empty.

—Vera my Vera, where are you! he shouted.

He fell to his knees and set his head against the side of the box, then rose up and looked within again.

—I also will go, he said so only he could hear, and lay down in the box as well.

For Linus the box was too short and he was forced to bow his knees so he would fit.

He closed his eyes and hoped that he would soon be lost, and then one day later found again, deep underneath.

no. 32

At the picnic, Vera kissed Linus on the cheek as he laid the blanket out beside the child's hand. It had not shriveled at all, this hand, or been changed by the weather.

—God loves a child, remarked Linus.

Vera poured the wine.

Vera and Linus stood on the beach early in the morning holding hands. They saw a glimpse of the island far away.

—Will you come with me? asked Linus.

Vera kept silent for a time. Then she gave Linus a hard look.

—Only if you bring me an eye before day ends. If you do, I shall go with you on the morrow.

❋

Later this same day, Linus brought Vera a greenish-blue eye.

—This is for you. It is from the ocean, he said and laid it cautiously in Vera's palm.

She took a careful look.

—This eye reminds me of a vaguely blue color that I saw one evening when I was a child.

And she held it near her breast with a dreamy countenance from far away.

Vera and Linus took themselves to a house on the edge of a long wasteland.

We shall learn a craft, said Linus, and it will support us through all the days of this life.

We shall learn a craft, said Vera, and there will be bread on the table, and also pheasant and also goose. There will be a table and on the table there will be these things.

In the house there was one small window looking towards the waste and one window looking away.

This, said Vera, is the homeward window. She used chalk to draw two goats standing like men. They went together to the homeward window which was the window facing the road home.

Vera said later to Linus, of this and other moments in their life,

—I gained suddenly the ability to double myself. Vera, your Vera, was in the house, sketching the goats, preparing a place and a life. But another Vera went out into the salt waste and walked many hours fraught beneath the sun until she came to a wooden door set in a small hillock set itself in the featureless expanse.

—I did not knock on the door, said Vera. I saw immediately it was the way out, and I was not ready yet to go.

An old man sat on a chair in the corner. His hands were tied behind his back and the lips were bone-dry. His face was all pale and the body shivering.

—Soon the evening comes and then I will sing you a song, said Vera. That will be nice, no?

She looked at Linus who stood in the doorway opposite her.

—But you must though be thirsty, my love, she said.

Linus smiled.

A low murmur came from the old man. The shiver increased.

—Will you have some water? she asked.

—Yes thank you. That would be nice, said Linus.

Vera walked slowly to him, then a kiss on the cheek and a leaving of the room.

A while later she returned with a full glass of water and a walking across the floor. She stopped in front of the old man and stood still for a moment holding the glass while his eyes got bigger. He began to convulse.

Vera spilled the water down in front of him. There came a piteous noise that resembled a dog's howl, and Vera let the empty glass fall.

—Why did you do that? Linus asked sorely. You knew it was the water I wanted.

—Oh, forgive me, my heart.

She went to him and they embraced.

—Forgive me.

A day and a day and a day and then Linus found a craft to which he might turn his hand.

—Here, he said, showing Vera a spot on the forest path.

—We will wait here, he said, and when someone comes, we will swiftly waylay them.

—But Linus, said Vera, this is the road to the waste. No one comes along it.

—I will seek then, said Linus, another craft.

Vera stood by the open kitchen window and looked out. On the street two croaking seagulls were fighting over a loaf of bread. Their beaks closed over each other again and again.

Vera stretched her hand towards the window. Vera thrust all her fingers against the glass.

Linus sat by the table, a cup of tea in front of him. He put two lumps of sugar into it, all the while watching Vera out of the corner of his eyes. He was stirring very slowly indeed.

Vera watched how one of the birds prevailed and flew away with the bread, while the other went angrily about in the street and then disappeared behind a corner.

In the same breath there was a hard knock on the door.

Vera turned towards Linus, still with her fingers on the pane. They looked the one upon the other.

Finally, Vera spoke, drawing her hand back.

— The sun is shining.

— It is true, said Linus. The sun is shining.

Vera and Linus learned of a woman living then in the town. She was a sculptor of dogs and other tame animals. What do I mean by this? Well, she would break their legs and paws and muzzles and fuse them with other animal parts. In her yard, dogs with bird heads nosing in old snuff boxes for bits of thread with which to weave their enormous nests. In her pond, a duck with the body of a duck and the neck of a duck, but the cumbersome head of a bear. This last so delicate he could do naught but beg for crumbs and bits of fish. Oh, if you could hear the sound of his pleading!

Linus took himself to her fence and peered and peered. Vera too.

—Shall we hurt her? asked Vera. Shall we fuse her broken limbs to the limbs of another?

—Let us, said Linus,

and

—Yes,

and

—Dearly, I want to.

So they caught this woman in a net and pinioned her arms and severed them and killed a sea turtle with vile words and emptied it from its hardness and invested her there and then set her afloat with a sentence of several turtle lives to live. And oh, the oblivion, the long oblivion of a turtle life!

Linus broke a bottle on the floor and said to Vera
that each fragment of glass was a gift meant for her.

And this he said without knowing
what was hidden in her pocket.

Linus surprised Vera in her bath.

Linus had killed a man and was wearing his skin like a coat, with the skin of the face making a clever sort of hood.

—How Aztec! said Vera.

—I've had it drying in the barn at least a month, said Linus, and each day I go and rub ointment in to keep it supple. One wouldn't want to wear a rough and brittle skin-coat.

They looked at each other. Linus did a glad dance.

—Who was he? asked Vera. Where did you catch him?

—By the stream, said Linus. I was napping and he came with a question. By chance I had my skinning knife there in the grass at my side.

—What was his question? asked Vera.

—He wondered, said Linus, if I'd been sleeping long and whether I knew if it was to rain, and if so whether it would be very much.

—Sounds nice enough to me, said Vera. You might have let him go and waited for someone else.

—I could not, said Linus stiffly. I wanted his skin and now I have it.

—Anyway, said Vera. Let's go reconnoiter. As you

have a skin coat, I shan't rest until I have one as well. What sort do you recommend?

—A portly man, said Linus, of ample means and little foresight.

Vera had never been to this place before. There was a squeak in the hinges as they opened; inside it was completely dark. Linus took Vera's hand and led her onward one step and another.

—Have you ever touched a dead eye? he asked.

—No, said Vera.

—Would you like to?

—Yes.

Linus held fast her hand.

—Come with me.

He lead her until they came to a wooden door which Linus opened. Then up a steep ladder.

At the top, musty air and dampness. Linus still held tight to Vera's hand. He took her forefinger and pointed with it here and there until it touched something in the darkness.

It is cold and feels like a wet flower, Vera thought and breathed all she could.

And withal they dreamed first of a house in which they might live and built it night by night with the luminous labor of their sleeping minds.

One day — shall we go and find this place?

The dressing then in clothes prepared. The right hand road that may yet lead left.

A long while upon the road. They passed down through a glen, through a burrow and out a tunnel through a farrier's hut. In through a stable where sable mares drowsed beneath unkempt gables.

With a wink and a clapping of hands, with small leaps afoot, they came to a small hill and atop the hill, this dreamed place.

—Shall we live here, asked Linus, so far from what we know?

—There's nothing dear to you in the piles of the known, my Linus, said Vera.

And she was wrong, but he believed her.

Settle here, settle here, called the house.

Drowse you too, called the stable, and the hill, and the road.

The path is gone, said the farrier's hut, departing.

And they were left there then, with the day paused as though upon one's outstretched fingers.

Vera and Linus knew of a woman in the district who delighted in torturing her dog. She would starve him for many days until he hardly could walk, and then pretend to strangle him with a wire before eventually laying some morsel of food before him.

Also, a couple of weeks ago, she shaved off all his fur so he most resembled an enormous mouse.

Vera and Linus kept the woman under observation for several days, and thus found out that every morning she walked the same way to the market with her dog. Thus equipped, they made appropriate plans.

One morning they waited for her to leave the house, and then followed her a little distance without her noticing.

When she took a certain turn into an empty narrow street, they attacked her from behind and drew her into an abandoned basement.

The dog crouched in the corner and Vera and Linus tied the woman's hand and feet.

Linus took up his knife and thrust it against the skin of the woman's neck while explaining to her what it meant to give such animals bad treatment. Then he cut her open, slowly and rather shallowly.

Afterwards Vera and Linus left her there lying on the floor with the innards peering out. How gentle they were, carrying the dog away wrapped in Linus's coat!

Linus kissed Vera. She patted his cheek.

Then, with a little

—HA!

she slashed his hand with a straight razor.

Blood beaded along the shallow cut.

Linus held his hand delicately with his other hand.

—Can you guess, asked Vera, can you guess what I'm going to do now?

Vera and Linus went together to the house of a man who was very sick, indeed dying, of an illness he had contracted as a young man while traveling in the SUDAN. They entered his low lying far flung house. First was the kitchen, a small tidy affair. Next was the bedroom. The bed was empty, and it seemed no one had lain there for some time. Into the bathroom, then, they went. No one was there either.

—Where, asked Vera, is your friend?

She lifted up an old hat. Underneath was a cocked pistol from the battle of El Alamein.

—Where, asked Vera, is your friend and mentor who even now is dying of a sickness he contracted years ago as a young man traveling in the SUDAN?

—John Rupert Digham! shouted Linus. COME OUT, COME OUT!

But there was no answer. Sad to say, so little is known of the disease that many years before John Rupert Digham, a young man, traveling in the SUDAN, had contracted, that we cannot here describe with any precision its progression.

## Only this:

1. First one is bitten by a small mouse-like creature of no account.

2. One forgets the incident. The bite is inconsequential, is hardly felt; even when felt, the bite is disregarded by the active intellect — such a mouse, what

harm could it do? one thinks, and goes on with one's business.

3. One cultivates one's life, one's friends, one's means, one's hopes. One goes from place to place, from triumph to triumph, in search of ambition and ambition's remedy as though in flight across some imagined map, the subject of a conversation in a comfortable English room.

4. Precisely, after an exact parcel of time somehow embedded deep within the teeth of the mouse itself, the trap springs shut. One falls deathly ill. One takes to one's bed. One closes the windows, fastens the shutters. Within, darkness, stale feel of wallpaper and old sheets. What has one done with the time one had?

5. Not death, really, but a slow fading as friends come and go. Progressively the greetings and farewells tire one more and more. One feels perhaps it would be better to have no visitors. The doctors agrees. The doors are bolted.

6. One disappears completely out of the bed, out of the locked room with fastened shutters. Clever friends come calling after the doctor and servant have made off can find no evidence of anything that occurred, so swiftly and so slowly did death's strategy unfold.

Yes, like a pincushion held gently beneath the tongue of a marionette, so careful you have been, and yet all was for naught.

—Let us each take something, said Vera, to remember him by. I will take this.

She took a Zulu spear and shield from the wall.

—If it must be, said Linus.

He took a leather flask from a hidden cavity behind a painting of Cromwell.

—A sleeping potion! said Vera, with a hiss.

But Linus shook his head.

Vera and Linus were walking along a narrow path.

A little bird came flying and landed in front of them. Vera and Linus stopped to take a look at him, and at that he came closer, all up to their very feet.

— Follow me, he said and flew in between the trees.

They followed him for a while until they came to a sort of hole in the rock.

The bird then flew away.

— Fare thee well, my friends!

Vera and Linus stood still and looked inside. It seemed large enough for a body to fit through.

— Who do you think lives in the cave? Linus asked, intent on Vera.

– I think it is our shadow, she said, and a smile came onto her face.

Vera wrote a poem that could compel her.

She gave the poem to Linus
and required a similar verse from him.

—In the night, all things go awry, she said. It shall not be so with us.

—Let's go for a walk, said Linus.

—Let us, said Vera. And shall we bring the head along?

—A fine idea!

Linus fetched it from the shelf. With the head under his arm, he followed Vera out into the world.

After walking for a long while, they halted in front of a dark painted door of great size.

—No, not here. I won't. I just won't! the head shouted.

—Yes! Certainly, you come with us, said Vera with a hard fixed manner of smiling.

—But I don't want to, the head whined. I won't.

Linus rang the doorbell. They waited by the door and all the while the head kept on contradicting everything they said.

Finally the door opened. In front there stood a woman with a strict countenance that twisted into a grimace of disgust when she saw the head beneath Linus's arm.

—We wish to return this, said Linus.

The woman snatched at the head with a loud cry. The head shouted too. Slam! and the door was shut. Vera and Linus stood there quietly, alone, listening.

Vera was alone walking in the forest. In the bushes she caught sight of a rabbit stooping by a large stone and reading from an old book.

—What are you reading?

The rabbit looked askance at her. After some time it deigned to speak.

—This is a story about elves and hidden people who live their lives inside rocks like this one.

It closed its eyes and turned its head back towards the book.

—Can you read with your eyes closed? Vera asked in surprise.

—Of course.

Vera felt the rabbit wishing she was gone.

—Goodbye, said Vera.

—Yes, goodbye.

The rabbit still had its eyes closed. But then it opened them and looked on Vera.

—Perhaps one day we will meet.

—Perhaps, said Vera and strode off.

Said Linus,

—Like a bird that arrives at a house and must first remove its wings before entering, I am astonished by the sudden nearness of voices.

Vera climbed up a high and graceful tree. But just when she had reached the highest and most elegant branches, she looked at the ground. A great dizziness came on her, and she would not dare come down.

—Linus, Linus! she shouted. I am stuck! I can't come down!

—Stay calm, he answered. I will come up to you. This will be all right.

And Linus started climbing up the tree. It took him longer than Vera, but finally he came to the upper reaches where Vera sat.

—Now everything is fine again, he said and put his arms around her.

—Now we are both up here. Together.

Vera and Linus undid the ropes that were wrapped and tied around the tree at the cliff edge. So suddenly the ropes shot away!

Vera's fingers were burned.

And Linus, by the cliff edge:

—Now they are falling. Now they are falling. Now they have gone among the rocks.

Then Vera and Linus went with a great canvas sack and gathered the parts from among the rocks.

What did they do with this bag of limbs?

I suppose you would like to know, and although I had every intention of telling you when this story began, I find that your manner has become now so impertinent that I am compelled not only to leave the room, but further, to consider in passing whether or not I should cut you in the face with the razor blade I carry in my pocket, so then to leave a lasting scar. You won't be so insolent then, will you?

Linus found a hole in between moss-grown stones.

—Let's put something in this hole, he said to his Vera.

—Sure. What shall it be?

—Perhaps a nice little stone, he said. Or a message from ourselves to whomever finds it.

Linus discovered one day a little book about Vera's past. It related that Vera had been a tightrope walker in a sprawling hypnotic eastern city before dying violently in a pogrom.

—How did you come to be here? he asked her later that same day.

—Why, said Vera, I paid someone else, a servant girl in the palace, to die in my stead. Then I fled the city in a golden coach drawn by wicked children.

—But what did you pay her? asked Linus.

—Rubies, said Vera. Rubies from the long calling gardens of the sun.

In a small house there lived an old man among books and a cat. The house was old and ramshackle, but the man had been living there many years without even his wife who had passed away and left him all alone. He had no friends beside the cat, and did hardly leave the house except for buying food and other necessities. His time passed in reading.

One day when the old man opened the front door for checking the mailbox, a little box sat on the doorstep. He took it up and opened it to find eight pieces of chocolate. How astonished he was!

Back into the house he went, holding the box in his hands like a fragile treasure. And closed the doors.

This was Thursday.

A week later new-baked bread awaited him along with a fine can of tuna. The latter this man gave to the cat.

And from then on, a Thursday morning never came and went without the man finding a new treat on the doorstep, sometimes a parcel of food, sometimes an object. And sometimes a little poem or a story, written with peculiar handwriting that he could never recognize.

Linus picked Vera up.

He took her and plunged her head in water.

—Have a little death, he said. For I am to bake a pie tonight and there must be death in the house.

A bird that Vera caught and tied to her ankle.

Another tied to Linus's.

Then, a foot race down Elkin Street.

Who will win?

—Not I, but the other, says Vera, whose bird has escaped her and even now vengefully crosses the sky in long circles, nursing its fifteen broken wings.

This day it was pouring rain with stark coming of thunder and lightning.

Vera liked to hear the rain banging the shutters and the roof. She listened by the open window and imagined that she was out in the open sea aboard a man-of-war. The ship was rocking furiously, and suddenly there was increase of thunder and lightning, increase of rain.

The enemies had begun their attack.

—Linus, Linus! she called. They have begun to fire!

Linus jumped up.

—We have to go up to the deck and fight! she shouted.

She took Linus's hand and they sought the weapons. Then they set off running.

They climbed the steep ladder. They opened the little door.

They went together out into the pouring rain, girded for battle, grimaces upon their wet faces.

Linus looks up from his lifetime of work as an undersecretary in the Department of Implausible Devices and Vera is standing there, newly come from a wooden crate shipped in haste across the border.

She is a bit shy. All of this is new to her.

—Excuse me, she says. Is this the Department of Implausible Devices?

In answer, Linus takes off his hat and arranges his hair in the manner of a jury of a wolves.

—But have you, asked Vera, seen this one?

With a snapping of buttons, her clothes are dismissed. Underneath Linus can see years of Thursdays, all in a row, with nary a Wednesday, a Tuesday, a Friday, a Sunday, a Saturday, a Monday between.

—How did you do that? howled Linus.

—I was always thinking of something else, said Vera, and wandering off. One day, in the midst of studying a book about trees, I had the clearest thought. I felt that I would die on a Thursday, and I saw myself then, in my last moments. The time between was negligible. I was a child and I was an old woman. I was dying and I was practically still being born. And now here I am again, stuck between.

They looked at each other in the crumbling light of a photograph hung upside down from a string.

Linus crawled up from the earth with the filthy face of an urchin.

—Come down here and take a look, he said.

Vera crawled down after him.

On the bottom there was space for them both, and they made themselves comfortable.

—Isn't this perfect? asked Linus. Now we are finally safe. No one will think to look here.

Vera and Linus took to the hills pursued by a great force of men and hounds.

Vera had offended someone with her bold speech. This had led to a reprisal of sorts in which Vera had been derided in a newspaper. Then Vera and Linus had burned the newspaper building to the ground, killing everyone inside. They had done this on purpose. No one can say that they did not know what they were doing. For just before doing it, Vera had said to Linus:

—Shall we burn them all to smithereens?

And Linus had nodded.

—We are arsonists, they afterwards related proudly, taking to the hills pursued by a great force of men and hounds.

A big black cat was sitting in the windowsill and staring at Linus.

—What is your will? Linus asked.

—I live here, said the cat.

—You live here?!

Linus was astonished.

—But I've never seen you before. How long have you been here?

The cat sat in the windowsill.

—For hundreds of years.

—And where did you come from?

The cat gave a sigh that spoke of centuries of fruitless questioning.

—I'm sorry, I can not talk about it.

—Besides ... you could never understand it, he added and looked away where Linus was not.

Vera woke in a comfortable warmth of darkness. She could not move her arms or legs. They were tight up against her. There was in fact very little air for her to breathe and that made her both drowsy and petulant.

—Where am I? she asked her grandmother's brooch.

—In a barrel, the brooch replied. You have been stuffed into a barrel, let loose of your life. Plunging down a river, you'll soon be gone away. Certainly, no one will remember you. Not in the least, not even pausing for a moment on the stairs before continuing.

A cruel woman was she, this grandmother of Vera.

For it is not pleasant either after a long life, to be stuffed wholesale into a brooch and be given to a child to wear.

They were out walking in evening in a place empty of people

and the moon was hidden.

Crooked trees sought for them while they followed

a path that would soon end.

And then the dark valleys.

Vera and Linus saw a girl reading poetry at a café in the centre. She was rather short with blond hair and wore a doll-like blue dress of dark spots. She introduced herself by saying that she had never before read from her own work, and her voice trembled as she spoke.

—How wonderful she is, so small and sweet, Vera whispered to Linus. I wish we could take her home with us and have her to sit on our sofa. That would surely make me happy.

—Then we shall, said Linus.

✿

When the reading was over they followed the girl, and when they got the chance, they grabbed her from behind and held her tightly between them while going home. She whined piteously and struggled at first. But she soon gave up, for their will was far stronger than hers.

At home Vera and Linus were greatly disappointed.

The girl looked everything but good in the sofa. After being placed there she started crying constantly and her face became red and swollen. Also, her blue dress was rumpled and wet.

—This is not working.

Vera was disconsolate.

—We have to return her.

—I've thought of something! said Linus.

He went into the storeroom and went furiously among a great quantity of tools. When he returned to the living room it was with a large butcher knife clutched in his hand.

He walked up to the girl and in one move he cut her open.

Then Vera and Linus started removing her innards, replacing them with all kinds of things —cotton, old garments and other useless things of their possession.

The task was difficult and would not finish until evening. But by then the girl was finally as Vera had imagined her to be.

—Finally, you are behaving as you are supposed to, said Vera.

The girl was sitting in the sofa quiet and sweet, so neat in her beautiful blue dress.

And she gave a little smile to Vera and Linus.

Vera turned away from the little tea party. The day was hot and the grass seemed to her full of sadness, as though life could never go very far before being called back. She thought then of Varsithon, Linus's hero.

And Varsithon, he knew how to command a troop of men. He knew how to give a building eyes, a tree hands. He knew how to come in great strength out of unlikely places, when all seemed lost in a riven occupied country.

And Varsithon, he brought the water out of the hills and besieged even the town of Yent with waves, though from its walls no sea was ever seen. All therein perished and he gave the land to his brother to rule.

And Varsithon became Emperor of the Air by a grand trick. He had gone on foot to the Devil and they spoke together, not in Hell, but in that far land on the far side of Hell, of which so little is reported or known.

—Shall I be Emperor of the Air? asked Varsithon, hearing all things through the eyes of birds, seeing all things through their beaks, passing all manner of time in the speed of clouds which seem so slow in the distance, but move, as we know, faster than horses or the bold fathers of horses.

—You shall be, said the Devil, Emperor of the Air, but you must give a thing to me.

—What, pray tell, may that be? asked Varsithon.

He stood up and walked to the very water's edge.

—What shall I give you? he said again.

—Bring me, said the Devil, upon a great wooden barge:

- the tails of a hundred cats
- the noses of three kings
- an apple grown by chance on a lemon tree
- a flock of tethered birds contained somehow yet still in flight
- the smallest grain of sand in all the Orient
- the mandibles of a mandarin beetle, insect that knows all things but speaks not
- the names of ten children who died before they could be named
- a flock of sheep dressed as scribes and trained in every clerical task
- a box of fingers kissed in parting by chaste lovers in elder days

And Varsithon brought these things and was declared and made for then and always

# Emperor of the Air.

—I would very much like to have your hair if you will cut it one day, Linus said to Vera.

—Certainly you can, she answered. If I should ever choose to cut it.

—But even if so, she added, … you, though, shall never have my eyes.

Faintly, she grinned.

+

Days passed and dark night, and Linus never got her hair.

Though, as all know, one day he got her eyes.

Linus crept out in the night to go and see about a garden he had laid in the cemetery of his devastated family.

He passed then along thin roads in beams of light like the glances of animals through leaves in Decembers of the fourteenth century.

A gate then in the dim air.

Linus thought of a stone and a river within a stone and a town beside the river. He began to think about it and he saw it vividly. He felt it rushing towards him. He could make out the steeple of the town, the tops of the houses. He saw faces in the street looking. He felt if he thought for even an instant longer about the town he would be lost in it and might never return.

And seldom can we arrive in the night without the vestiges of other beings, other needs troubling us.

We are strongest when alone, acting in legion as all that of which we are capable. Yet precisely thus we can be mistaken for nothing or less than nothing, a cloud of dust on the road, a darkening archive of filaments and silhouette.

This is some of what Linus felt.

And then with a jumping of fences he came to the garden.

Six stones in a circle, all written over with the lives of those who raised him. A tree long begun from red Japan, with the most elegant leaves, leaves like learned speech heard in passing upon a street one knows quite well one will never walk upon again.

Linus touched the dirt with his hands. He turned it over once, twice, as one turns a coin, for the garden loved him well, would do anything to please him, and above him the moon remembered this and that compact they had made, and cast for him an especial torchlight and sang even the quietest of river songs.

For though the moon is not a river, it is the mother of all rivers and the songs that rivers sing they learned long ago when the moon spoke and went about as you or I, though better.

Linus found a page from an old book buried in the depths of his death-garden:

—Behind the countryside there is another countryside, and behind that, a hallway. Strung along it, six doors. Pass first through the country, and then through its side. Then again through the second country. Pass then through a hill and to this graying hall, for there I have laid a place for you. A place and a feast, and the satin of gray gray morning for remaining where you will lie long.

And Linus knew then it was no hall, but a grave, not doorways but coffins.

—Who then has left this note? he murmured. He shall learn I am no fool.

Vera and Linus had a wager.

The loser was to wake early and lie upon the kitchen floor playing dead until the winner should come and wake the pretender to life again.

Linus lost the wager. The morning after, when Vera woke, he was as described upon on the floor.

She lay down beside him and told him a story of a boy who could not speak, and after the story she kissed him on the eyelids and whispered a few words in his ear. She took his hand and whispered the same again.

And again.

But without an answer.

The dark parade now and then in Vera's eyes.

She has gone from me, said Linus, swearing softly.

And Vera would go off to a stream, throwing off all her clothes, and she would bleed the stream and she would bleed the ground and she would bleed the sky and the air, so sharp were her shears, so sure her hand.

Over herself she would drape this blood and others still untold.

—I am queen in the absence of the queen, said Vera to herself.

And in the dream's depths, the true queen nodded.

AND Linus betook himself to write a METHOD for WAYLAYERS

# A METHOD FOR WAYLAYERS AND OTHER LIKE SORTS DEVISED BY L. FOR PRACTICAL USE

in 27 parts

A highwayman must know the land well. His knowledge of the land must exceed that of the law. He must know all routes and passages, all fords and passes in good weather and bad, all grottoes at all tides, high and low. He must learn the animals and their calls, all their hollows and impasses. Further, he must befriend at least one kind, that it may scout and flurry, to warn him of danger and fortune impending.

A highwayman must carry a weapon or be himself a signal danger with his hands. By this last I do not mean a willing boxer or brawler. I mean capable of the severity of mind necessary for the wrenching of necks, the bursting of throats and eyes.

We are not of the opinion that threat of word alone compels; the waylayer's sovereignty is achieved through example and reputation. Bodies must at some time be the proof of his serious nature.

∧

To speak of the last made thought — these bodies must be chosen with care and delicacy at first, so as not to provoke any great attention on the part of the populace. We do not advise the casual slaying of any individual whose death will incite the law to rise up from sleep and hound the waylayer from hill and dale, kith and kin. Victims should be chosen in the first months of advent by their own whereabouts-of-dislike. A cruel landowner, a foreign traveler, etc. Someone not to be missed.

^

The effect on one's reputation of unnecessary killing is delightful. Those waylaid become the soul of courtesy, offering up all their riches with ease and candor. One hasn't lived until one has ridden the KING's road as a devil-taken-waylayer. Oh, the deference one is shown!

^

A waylayer must dress well, speak well, be, in fact, a master of speaking, of dancing, of writing, of painting. In short, a gentleman, though we require no article of birth. For the waylayer ascends a ladder of merit and will. Forcefulness, not in society, but on its edges! Such is the way.

The waylayer must have in his keeping a hold or hideout, a safehouse hidden beyond sight. The way there must be obscured and difficult, yet simple for him. There must be a room there for the storing of all manner of wealth — even down to a stable for horses (and dare we say the occasional elephant or ox?). There must be in the safehouse a sufficiency of all that the waylayer requires such that he may stand any length of siege or trouble. For the land may in time turn against him. Poor favor overcomes even the great, as we know from the Romans. One must be prepared.

And indeed for such as we, such times are best. It's then we can attend to our perfections, to the gaining of physical strength, of mental celerity. Shall we grow swift? Shall we be quick to climb and leap? Shall we comprehend the things we read in stirring breadth? Yes, breadth: breadth of thought, of forethought. A great reading of books, a great planning of futures, both one's own and those in the near world. A casting of the cards. A saying of names.

The highwayman must have a servant of unquestionable cleverness and hope. This must be a man or woman of that peculiar sort who has set his or her life to the perfection of a life within a life — that is to the perfection of a servitude. He must be happy in his lot, wishing for nothing more than to keep one's domicile. This individual must pride himself on the venture of your paired lives, must consider himself tied to you by more than blood. In short, all the old ideas of duty must burn in the hollows of your servant's mind.

FOR TOO IT IS THIS SERVANT UPON WHOM YOU MUST RELY IN SICKNESS, IN INJURY AND IN NECESSARY SEQUESTERINGS.

∧

The servant's ties to the near town must be inviolate and safe. How else the gaining of food and wants in all seasons and times without danger or suspicion?

The servant must be of a particular type. He must be the sort of man who is adamant and inconceivably correct in his sphere. He must be the sort from whom one goes in gladness after a momentary meeting, the sort whose belongings have a sheen of careful use. You, you might think upon seeing him, could never use any tool, any item, so thoroughly or well. And yet we are speaking of a glove! of a boot! of a map or whistle! Do not mistake me in this. I do not speak of grace or beauty, but simply of delightful efficacy. How splendid must be this man's simplicity of manner. He would never allow you into his quarters, or at least, you would never ask it, and he would never offer. But how finely arranged must be his simple things! To see this man hang a coat upon a hook, to see him stand in his shirtsleeves at his small window gazing down along the road …

His is the strength that will deliver you again and again. And yet he is but your servant. You may say things lightly to him and he must obey. In deed, he will take a pride in obeying all that you say, and will not, as some do, argue back or say what he thinks is the best course. Such suggestions or thoughts as may come to him will be delivered to you in letters that he will write and leave upon a table. His writing will be simple, with poor lettering and horrible grammar, despite the clean efficiency of his tongue. Nothing worthwhile will be communicated to you by his letters.

And yet, they will allow you to know that he has had some thought regarding a matter, a thought of exceeding coherency. Then you must plumb him for this thought, while laboring at his side in some manner, perhaps walking to observe the mason's work on the orchard wall, or in martial practice.

For it is he ( have I said it not?) who will be your partner in the drills of hand and foot that will keep you strong in your confinement.

∧

Shall we speak of the frequency of attacks?

Often enough that one may consider oneself employed.

Seldom enough that the road is kept to by travelers. Seldom enough that the travelers go undefended.

One must work against the patterning of habit. Keep a carpet or arabesque hung upon the wall and place there in your eye the occasions of your waylaying. Count them upon the lines and in the changing colors. When you see any vein of predictable action, halt it! Halt it by all means! Never let yourself fall prey to a guarded caravan whose foreknowledge of your timed attacks allows them any advantage. Those you choose shall have no advantage at all, save the advantage of your acquaintance thereafter. But, of course, I jest. A wrapped cloth about your face will keep your life intact, unknown, unblemished.

Yet in your heart we must not let this small insult pass unaddressed. There is no blemish in our lonely fraternity. I only spoke of what others might think.

∧

Keep a memory of all places where a waylaying took place. Do not repeat until some number has passed, say thirty, say fifty, fetching-aways.

In the event of capture, know you the ways of ropes and locks. Know you too the science of persuasion, for more malleable than rope or lock is the mind of your captor. Force them by your skilled speech to plug the ears of your guards, to proscribe their actions. Then, though imprisoned, you in your turn will have imprisoned them.

In the person of your known-name, be irreproachable and grave. Be grave to the point of deadliness. This is to say, discourage any slight, aspersion or suspicion by acting in many duels and silencing (in the known sphere) a sufficiency of men to prohibit any easy investigation into your affairs. Only at great cost must such an undertaking pass.

^

Consider the wife, the husband of your servant. Best of all perhaps is an old, or, if young, infertile couple. For children draw loyalty away from you, cause the minds of your servants to tend towards another object. Bind your servants to you by filling all needs. In this way be you a servant to your servant and a servant to your own desired secrecy and closeness.

There is a story about a badger that goes like this:

A badger was departing one day from the house of a friend. He had passed down along the path from the door some ways when he remembered he had forgotten his stick. He returned to the door, but slowly, being in the middle of a long thought (such as badgers are known to have). When he reached the door, he did not knock upon it, thinking it better simply to procure the stick from the inner hall and make off without another round of greetings and farewells. But, no sooner did he start to inch the door open than the door was thrown wide.

—YOU AGAIN! bellowed his host. Haven't we had enough of you for one day! You come here, eat our food, drink our good berry-wine. You come here and laze around in my best chair, talking nonsense about the world of the Sidh, which you say is just beyond sight. You grouse, you gambol, you mince, you mutter. Sir, I say, we have had just a bit too much!

What followed then is too sad to relate. Leave it to me to say that no one profited from this violent encounter, least of all the host, for an angry badger is a dangerous proposition, even a bookish one, whether with or without stick.

So, the moral of that is, keep a tiny window at knee level from which you can watch people come and go. Most certainly you will find it useful.

^

Have it known that you yourself or your servant has been waylaid by the highwayman you know yourself to be.

Perhaps, have your servant pose as the highwayman, and have yourself and others together in company waylaid by same. Then, those you prey upon will come forward as your witnesses — surely he cannot be the waylayer, they will say. Why, wasn't he waylaid with us beside him?

∧

Be of good fortune in word and deed. Make it so that no one may suspect you — for you are so notably kind, for you are so splendid, so dear. To suspect you would be to question a tract of moral hope. THEN you will be unreachable.

^

In your approach to a stopped carriage or group afoot, show no hesitation. Use the old Chinese method of mask-switching in order to sow unrest and indeed unreasonable fear throughout your prey. Show no hesitation, sir. I say, show no hesitation. Force all to give you a genuine and thorough respect. Anyone crossing this simple line will be immediately killed.

To speak of the killing, it must be done in such a way that no one could possibly understand or relate thereafter precisely how it happened. This may seem difficult, but it is not. People in general have miserable memories. Their minds are weak and untrained. On the other hand, everyone remembers everything they ever saw and can relate for instance, the landing of a butterfly upon a hound's tooth coat while traveling through a park as a child in extreme old age moving like the means of a photograph across the scene, alighting here and there. I say strike suddenly, without any warning, and no one will understand how what you did could possibly have come to happen.

Any plot hatched in the town or among those of influence involving the improved policing of the roads, the setting of sentinels, bell-stations, warning fires, or the hunting down of the (unknown) waylayer, must be met with by your public persona. Contrive a circumstance in which the operative individual may be compromised or killed on behalf of honor. Otherwise, poison or vice may be employed. But, as we have noted, duels are far better. If the individual is an old man, do not fear to put in place the old handicaps: fight with a bound arm, a blindfold, or a much blunted sword, a weighted boot. Fight sword against pistol, for instance. It is a little known fact that in only four of the seventy-three duels ever fought at these stakes did the pistoleer succeed in putting his bullet through his adversary. Indeed, as you may have observed for yourself, again and again, against chance itself, men have attempted these odds. The reason for the failure is that to try and shoot a pistol against a man with a sword is a difficult thing. You are aware that if you miss you will not have time to reload, and that therefore you will be skewered. Without a doubt you will be skewered. And yet the hot action of battle does not sway you to great deeds of marksmanship, as in fact, no battle, nothing has passed yet. You are merely standing, pistol in hand and gazing down the barrel at a man with an unsheathed sword. The action of firing is a quiet task, a task of inanimacy. Tasks of inanimacy are, as we know, derailed entirely by the presence of a man with a sword. For instance, imagine trying to write a list for the grocer's while over you there stands such a frightful character. No, no, it cannot be done. And so, many have in their own pulling of the trigger, con signed themselves to death. And they are now dead. Those four of the seventry-three who succeeded were, as history tells us, not men to be trifled with. They were great hazard takers, and, instead of thinking of the danger of missing, they basked in the certainty of execution. One thought, I shall put this bullet through the young man's head, and then retire to the library for a bit of tea and a game of billiards. Another considered a bird and the eye of a bird upon a near branch. For him another man seemed to be shooting the pistol. That man did not miss. The third was a lunatic and cannot really be counted. His hands were bound in a strait jacket. He managed the pistol with his feet and mouth. What he was thinking at the time, who can say? He wrote after of the incident, once he had been installed as a dancing master in the court of King James the II: I may or may not have held the pistol with my feet and activated the trigger with my sinuous tongue. I may or may not have aimed for the back of his head, solely the back mind you, though the front was plainly first to come. The fourth of the four, as I shall tell you, was a woman in the guise of a young soldier. She was given the odds on the basis of her physical weakness. However, her force of will was such that she actually managed to convince her opponent that she had already fired, and that the pistol had failed to go off. When her opponent came closer, she shot him point blank, a much easier task.

One must speak clearly and well to those one overtakes upon the road. To crimes of theft one must add no crimes of a moral or incourteous nature. One must be noted for one's manners and speech to such a degree that, though it would never come to pass, one might be thought easily of as a proper tutor to youth in all that is good and right. BY ONE's GOOD BEHAVIOR, one must prompt a reinvestigation into whether or not it is actually wrongdoing to waylay travelers. Perhaps, cause them to think, it is only the natural order of things. THEN YOU WILL HAVE WON.

If you do not wish to cultivate a public persona, then have in the town some confederate of note, a friend perhaps from childhood, who will act as described on your behalf, dueling and fouling up any organizing of attempts against you.

Learn to speak the dialects of the mountain villagers. It may be needful in a dire pass to retire there.

For instance, one walking upon the road came to a path he had never seen before. A low stone wall went with him for perhaps a mile as he walked, and yet he did not look over it, despite every indication that to look over the wall would be a fine and joyous thing to do. Now why do you think he didn't look over the wall? It seems there was a muskrat rustling about in the leaves and carrying a letter from the late Emperor of China. This letter spoke of a certain peculiar circumstance that had arisen in the Imperial Court, the which could only be resolved through the use of an almost incomprehensibly distant emissary. The letter spoke of how various manners of gaining such an emissary had been discussed, and that, ultimately, the final decision had been made to birth the offspring of a man and a snake in an egg. However, the first three children born this way all exhibited similar characteristics of disdain and inconstancy. Finally, a very old man, far older even than the rock that stands in a pillar at the ford of Taip, came to the court carrying a tiny round bird. This bird, he said, can speak all languages, and knows several things we do not know. Let it be our messenger to seek after an emissary. And so the little bird flew and flew in its roundness across this ocean and that ocean, finally coming to a particular land of mountainous fastness, and there it alighted and spoke at length with a muskrat. The muskrat then took himself to a writing table and constructed the requisite letter. Thereafter he went looking for the proper fellow.

And he has found you! Taking up the letter you read the contents. The Emperor's wife does not believe in days other than the present day, neither tomorrow nor yesterday. Thus, she is invulnerable to argument, as argument relies for its rewards upon the future, and for its proof upon the past. How shall we convince her to go with us to the blossoming orchard and sit where the sun is most affectionate, in the wind-blown gladness of the highest turrets of this farthest, oldest sanctuary, place even the waters of the flood failed to cover?

Act to ruin other routes that might cause a decline in passage along your favored haunt.

For instance, lay all manner of dead animals in the road. Do this every morning of the year. How confusing it will be to those who travel there!

How can this eagle have impaled itself on the hoof of that cow? How can this horse have been turned inside out?

Certainly, no one will go willingly to such a place. In this, you can see, I am correct and have thought well and long for no small time. Certainly it has been the occupation of many of my waking hours, these past years, to think at length on the subject and come to definitive conclusions about how best to halt progress along roads.

So, I say, sever the head of a bull and rest it on a man's shoulders. Sew the two together and leave them there upon the road.

Then, sew the man's head to the bull's body, and fill it up with cogs and wheels such that it can be ridden comfortably. Go you then upon that road occasionally, selling little flails and bone-ornaments. Smudge your face with berry-juice or tar first as a precaution. You must not be recognized.

Assign to yourself some period of years at the end of which your actions will cease. At that time, you will have amassed enough wealth to perpetuate yourself indefinitely.

If excitement is what you seek at such a time, do not let it lead you again into becoming a waylayer. For you that time will have passed.

Instead, lead bands to hunt those who waylay others upon the public roads. With your knowledge of the trade, you should be expert in such ministrations.

And, while you are a practicing highwayman, look out for these very bands spoken of above. No respectable waylayer would ever be caught by such. Yet these bands do a great service to the expert waylayer by keeping the roads clear for him to act and thieve.

^

Never show mercy once your intent to kill has been shown. Of all weapons, your will is the strongest and most thorough. Let it flash, impend and let action swiftly come. No good can come of reprieve.

For instance, there was a man who spoke kindly to those he waylaid, and they became confident because of this. One found a pistol in the coach while his back was turned. Another shouted for distraction, and in the ensuing melee, our kind highwayman was shot to death. What reward that?

A grouse was watching, and it spoke to another grouse several yards distant. That grouse conversed with a fellow grouse in turn distant by some yards. In time this tale passed up and down the land, changing as it went, so that even you or I, hearing it now, can scarcely say whether or not we have heard it before.

Exchange your take with a merchant in a nearby city. Disguise this as some profitable albeit esoteric trade (that will give a reason to your seeming shiftlessness). You must not risk the use of stolen resources in the place where those goods were taken.

The painting of the eyes of dolls was the highest art of the Liu Dynasty of Ancient China. The dolls made then were treasured for centuries. Sadly, with the arrival of Confucius, and the spread of his edicts and precepts, all such things were destroyed. The danger that Confucius saw was a clear one: did not any who behold the dolls' eyes fall to talking only of that, to dreaming only of that, to sitting and staring into empty space, imagining a life within that wood or porcelain skull?

The best of these eye-makers was a man known as the Three Cloud Smith. His work so far outstripped that of his contemporaries, who themselves loom above any who followed, that he was accorded a mythic status. It is said his prestige was such that the entire district in which he lived was governed strictly according to a complicated pattern of movement so that he would always behold a particular woman by a particular bridge upon his daily walk, so that he would always see out this window or that window, a farmer taking his ease upon a set wall, leaning upon a set branch, or working, be it night or day, over a given patch of ground.

The hypnotic powers of these dolls were thought limitless, and, indeed, guards that surrounded Three Cloud

Smith's district halted any export of his creations. The Emperor was his only client, and for that, Three Cloud Smith was given a life of making in an eased landscape.

Be of good cheer. Rise in the morning with gladness in your heart. Stab with a knife in the same kind way. Prepare yourself for those with killings in dreams. Dream relentlessly the same road, the same caravan. Come again and again down the graded slope, fists gathered beneath an obscuring cloak. Is it a score you have left for dead these many nights? You must kill forty in dreams for each one in life.

^

Keep a record of all your waylayings and lock it in an ironbound chest buried at the foot of an oak. Write of this to your cousin in the distance beyond three oceans and four seas, saying, I too determine the manner of my tale. For nothing abides like a secret life. And all things return from beyond the sea, just as one who steps behind a screen will again step out. Those who speak of the world's great size have never seen it. Maintain your tale by stretching it past all geography. There was a word for this once in a tongue of pilgrimage. Doubtless it has been forgotten. So many of the words I long to speak have been forgotten! Might there be, unknown to me, one word that means all I hope, all I long for, all of that at once? Were I to hear it, I would faint, so perfect would be the address, so perfect the name.

AND SO,

Linus bound his METHOD in a book of skin and set it upon a shelf in his house.

—You may read it, he told his guests, but you must first cut your hand with the knife provided.

AND INDEED, tied with string to the pale volume there was a knife of exceeding sharpness.

Shall we say, there were many who went this way pleasingly, bleeding themselves to read the good book?

And out went Vera and Linus with a large knife and a bag, for hunting children's hands.

Finding children was easy and they cut left hands of twenty, and right hands of twenty more, since they found it unkind to leave someone alone with no hands at all.

Then they made the bag fast with rope.

At home they left the hands several days in the sun.

And when they were dry and stiff Vera and Linus took them inside and made from them a makeshift wind-chime.

—We shall always know now, said Vera, if a visitor is at the door.

Vera and Linus stood upon the cliffs listening to the calmness that some call the ocean. In between the waves they heard weak and sad voices from drowned children.

—How sad this is, said Vera. Let's throw stones to them so their hopes will improve.

They each found a stone correct for the filling of thoughts. These they cast into the sea, and the voices grew fainter and fainter as the stones sank to the bottom.

Vera woke in the afternoon. She was standing in the shallows of an enormous lake.

A bird with dark plumage and an overlong sparse tail had been desperately soliciting her aid for some quarter of an hour. Just as she woke it drowned and was lost.

—What can this mean? asked Vera. Have I lost at last the speech and thought of my childhood days?

—Or is there then some other more subtle explanation?

Then all at once, the lake subsided and she stood instead in a gown that spilled out across seven courtyards.

The bird had risen and was there again.

—It will take, said the bird, seven hundred courtiers seven days to lift and carry your train even so far as that window.

Vera walked upon the street. Linus was in a window on the highest floor of a building, looking down to her. With her hand she waved to him.

Then Linus was missing from the window.

Vera kept on looking up, calling and calling Linus's name in the hope that he would reappear. But in the same breath a little dark bird flew down from the roof, taking the path that Vera would.

And heavily he flew.

Linus reached under Vera's dress and discovered that beneath her stockings and beneath all her thin fabric, her legs were made of straw. He tore open her dress. Her hips were straw. Her chest was straw. Straw, her throat. Her head was scarcely recognizable.

—Vera, he cried.

And Vera stepped out from behind a curtain.

—Let us burn ourselves in effigy, she said.

And in her arms was a straw Linus, correct in every regard.

Linus was once walking alone in the forest when he came upon an old woman whose nature was that of a witch though no one could know this to look at her. She gave herself to speech and soon overcame him with hypnotism.

Then she set a crown of bone on his head and that was that. Linus had to obey her.

When Linus did not return from the woods to his Vera, she began to suspect what had happened for she had heard tell of the witch and the slave crown. Furthermore Vera knew that the only way to free Linus from the spell was to give him a human heart.

But she knew also that the person who did so would be changed into a cat when a day had passed.

Vera began to hunt for a heart for her Linus.

She considered at length what sort of heart would be best, and came to the conclusion that best would likely be a child's heart rather then an adult's. This because a child is an easier prey, and also because the heart would then be young and fresh, a good thing by any account.

She went off early in the morning to stroll in town limits and procure a child.

Around noon she caught sight of a little boy playing alone on a grass lawn with a ball. She felt he was correct for her purpose.

She watched him for a while, standing beside a housewall. And then she called to him saying that she had something he should like to see.

The boy came to her full of curiosity, and she beckoned him on. When he came close enough she set him up against a stone-wall, drew her knife and cut out his heart neatly and carefully, and from it gained the promise of Linus's freedom.

It was night and the weather held still.

Vera went into the forest disguised as a small tree.

When she came close to Linus's demesnes, a cave in the woods, she was moving calmly and slowly in the hope of escaping his notice for under the witch's spell he was quite likely to attack and even kill her.

But she did not see him on the path or in the woods, and when she reached the cave she found him asleep.

In front of the cave, Vera took off her disguise.

Then she went to where Linus was lying. Gently she laid the human heart in Linus's hand.

Immediately, he woke, freed from the spell.

At first he was utterly confused and didn't seem to realize at all what had happened. But Vera recounted to him everything about the witch and even about the danger they were possibly in now when the spell had been ceased. She also told him of the danger of becoming a cat the day after but Linus protested.

—That shall not happen my heart, he said.

And then Vera and Linus went together into the wooded darkness, and took of the night its promise for things that never end.

Vera went into a crowd as you or I would go into a house, but she went with a knife and took four eyes and an ear. This changed the crowd and it went with her thereafter east then west taking eyes and ears from those it crossed.

When Vera came upon Linus by the reservoir, she came down from the crowd, she came out of the crowd, she left the crowd and it sat first upon the ground obediently and then stood and then followed after her, nipping at her ankles and soliciting her love.

Linus came to Vera with a tiny piece of paper,
smaller than a fingernail, smaller than a drop of water.

—This for our love, he said

and set it upon Vera's outstretched hand.

Linus went to a little field and he made a ring of stones and sat then in it and thought and thought. When he was finished, he stepped out of the ring and back into his life.

Vera one day saw a sight that made her both deaf and blind. That lasted a day after which she was mute.

—Vera! Linus would say.

But she would say nothing in return.

—How shall I cure my Vera? asked Linus of himself.

And he decided promptly upon a course of action.

Linus went to the place in the forest where trees are felled and he sat there with Vera at his side.

—When the tenth tree falls, he told her, you will speak again and tell me what you saw.

Vera and Linus were vexed by a little lap-dog in their building who barked all the night and day. He interrupted their thoughts and one evening Linus had had enough.

—This has to stop! he said.

And late in the night when the dog had finally ceased its barking, they broke into the apartment where it lived. The damnable creature was fast asleep near the door, and its owner was asleep in a far room.

Vera and Linus broke the dog's neck and put the body into a brown canvas bag which they tied neatly with great satisfaction.

And early in the morning they went down to the shore with the bag.

They dug a deep hole in the sand and cast the bag in. Then they filled up the hole and stamped with their feet, stamped down and down while the sun was rising over the horizon.

Linus came upon a girl and a bird playing together.
First the girl was the bird. Then the bird was the girl.

—GOOD DAY, they said.

—Good day, said Linus.

—A RIDDLE, said the girl. HOW DID THE KID
DO A THING IT DIDN'T KNOW HOW TO DO?

—THE ANSWER IS IN A DREAM, said the bird.

And they went together away to God knows where.

Vera and Linus laid down a circle of conches
and broken sea shells by the strand.

But as they passed away along the shore road
they heard voices, children singing
of things lost, things buried for keeping.

Vera and Linus took themselves to a madhouse in order to visit Linus's uncle, once lunatic governor of Albrecht.

—Hello to you, said Linus.

—Once, said Linus's uncle, I had a chair in my chambers, a simple chair, caned in a pleasing manner. But in my power, my investiture as GOVERNOR, I told my servants, Anyone who sits in that chair is to be garroted.

With a thick pencil he drew a window on the smallest part of a large sheet of paper, then looked about as if to escape the gaze of the one who lived within.

—Yes, I have often been blamed for these garrotings. At my trial, many came forward and spoke against me. I say again now what I have always said in my defense: The sea weathers the land's edge into a cliff face over the course of centuries. In latter days, people settle in the vicinity. Some go walking there. If such a pair, in the full bloom of youth, were to perish by casting themselves thereof, then is the sea to be blamed for having carved the cliff to just that place? Say, by chance or unknowable dictate, the cliff edge was thirty feet farther. Would the lovers not have jumped to their deaths from there? The sea in this regard is found by all blameless. I ask only this clemency of the sea. Let I, who have weathered this cliff with my tides, with my night waters, let me be blameless too.

Vera thought it would be quite funny to fetch this chair out of the governor's palace and bring it to their little home in the fearsome wood. She paid a servant quite a sum to bring the chair to a back door and away she went.

Later that same day, Linus returned from a conclave of beasts. He came in the door, stripped off his animal-skin, removed his false head, and, preparing himself to take his ease, sat full down into a chair that had not been there the day before.

No sooner had he done so than a rope was fast about his neck, tightened and tightening. He struggled mightily, but Vera held the rope tight enough, and after a moment he collapsed completely.

—Who's more cunning now? asked Vera.

And she went off to bake a cake and boil water for tea.

—It will be ready when he wakes, said the candlestick who'd watched all the while.

Linus gave Vera a blue glass-bird.

—It's yours.

Vera made a place for it in an open drawer. Each day she took it up and held it carefully.

But one day the bird slipped from her and broke upon the floor.
In among the shards there was a note. It said:

—Between the walls it lies hidden and will never be seen until the sea rises high and the animals come to meet you. So be prepared!

Vera summoned all who were still living of those who had been oldest in the world to Linus when he was just a boy. On stretchers, on crutches, on canes, they came, and she bade them wait behind trees in a wood.

—Come love, she said, and took his hand.

To the spot they came.

OUT THEN, ALL AT ONCE!

—You are old, but we are older! they shouted. You can never grow so old as we!

And Linus wrested free of Vera and ran away through the trees to a hollow thicket where he hid his head and said many things to his clenched hands which I shall not by any means repeat.

Vera and Linus decided to break into a house in the middle of the night.

They'd heard the people were out of town, so the coast was clear.

They broke a window to reach the interior door-knob, and in they went. Then, they looked around going into all the rooms upstairs and downstairs, and finally to the kitchen to check the larder.

Such food was there! Linus began to cook in a broad pan with fine oil. Vera opened a bottle of red wine that she found and laid herself out on the table.

Soon the food was ready and together Vera and Linus sat down to eat.

They were of great appetite, and they ate with vigor and panache.
When the meal was finished Linus stood up. He held out a hand to Vera.

—Shall we dance? he asked.

And they danced in the kitchen as the hours thinned and thickened.

Vera and Linus came upon a winged creature in dark soil.

It was raging in the earth with its claw-hands, searching for something, but when it caught sight of Vera and Linus, it leapt up.

—What do you assume it's doing? said Vera.

—What are you doing? asked Linus.

The creature gave no answer. Perhaps it was dumb, as its mouth moved continually, but no noise came.

—Could it be an angel? Vera said contemplating the crumpled shabby wings.

—I think it is, said Linus in a reverie.

The creature had returned to its hunt in the soil and had ceased to worry over this imposition of Vera and Linus.

Vera took a step forward and then looked at Linus.

—Do you think angels feel pain? she asked.

—No. I am sure they do not, he said.

—Well that's good.

Then she drew her knife and went with determination to the beast. And thereafter returned to Linus with a pair of shabby blood-drenched wings.

Linus found a girl who was but an inch tall. She was perfect in every way, and spoke delightfully on many forgotten subjects with an erudition that was rightly astonishing. She was not shy at all, either, and removed her clothes at the slightest provocation to reveal a gorgeous, albeit diminutive form. Then how darling she was! Linus loved to wash her in a little porcelain cup and run the tip of his finger over her.

—Vera could never be jealous of one so small, he told himself.

Yet still he kept the girl a secret.

Then one day, Linus went to town to send a letter. When he returned, Vera was sitting in a chair facing the door. On the table in front of her was a glass turned upside down. Disconsolate, within it, was Linus's inchling.

Not a word then, not from Vera, not from Linus.

A cloud shaped like a gosling passed by. Then a cloud shaped like a deer.

Slowly Vera laced up her heaviest boots.

—Is it to be that way? asked Linus.

He drew a circle on the floor with a length of chalk.

Vera took the girl out from beneath the glass. Immediately she began to wiggle and try to escape. Vera tweaked her in the mid-section, and the little beast curled up.

Then Vera dropped it in the chalk circle where it lay and vomited.

Vera readied her foot to stamp.

—No words from me can move you now, that I know, said the tiny creature, but you are a damned pair and one day life will turn against you.

Vera took a hair from her own head and stuffed the entire thing into the girl's mouth until she could no longer speak. Muffled cries came through the hair gag. But the inchling did not run away, and it was later said by some it looked up at Vera's boot as it descended, looked up at the boot and recalled then the whole of her existence, from the blackness that was before to the blackness that would be ever after.

Vera walked into a hallway where there were four doors.

She went to the first, threw it open and looked inside. A fine dressed gentlewoman was sitting by a large oaken desk, and at her feet there was a little lap-dog. She was holding a pen and scribbling something in a little notebook, and all around there were vases of every conceivable kind and size.

The woman did not seem to notice Vera so she entered boldly. But as she came closer she noticed that the dog was impeccably unmoving and she wasn't sure if it was real. The woman chose that moment to speak.

—I'm sorry. We are closed, she said, and did not look up.

—Pardon me, said Vera.

She closed the door. Before her, another door.

Inside there was a couple sitting in a sofa, each holding a glass of wine.

—Cheers for the ocean! they said, also without seeming to notice Vera.

She closed the second, and opened the third door.

Inside there was an old man sitting in a rocking chair, so pale that he was nearly transparent.

Unlike the others he looked straight at Vera with fixed eyes.

—Within a while you will be given the key of the fourth door, he said slowly and his voice was hollow and without light.

If a dog were to learn to speak and stand in philosophical debate, how much of what we know would be overturned?

Vera and Linus had a wager where the winner should wait on a bench caught up with a blindfold while the loser would procure a treat.

Linus won and the following day he waited with eyes blocked until he heard Vera's voice singing him a little song. Then she took off the blindfolds to reveal a cinnamon cake in her outstretched hand with a candle in the middle.

—For you, she said and did a little dance of cinnamon-cake giving and blindfold removing.

Then Linus blew the candle.

On the seventh day
Vera was alone in the trees
having a funeral by herself.

It was quiet and dark
and no one could see.

Vera and Linus looked out a little window that Linus had drawn.

Outside three women were standing in the shadow of trees.

Each had a parasol, but the one in the middle now and then cast sidelong glances at the others.

—The one on the right has a parasol to fit in the group, said Linus. The one on the left does it to follow the fashion. But the one in the middle knows how ridiculous it is standing there in the shadow with parasols. It disgusts her and she is waiting for her chance to reach down to the pocket on her dress and show her followers what she really thinks of the whole thing once and for all.

Vera was, as we know, a prodigy in her childhood. Already at the age of seven, she had mastered the most difficult tricks and methods of diving. She was heralded as a great sensation. She toured the capitals of the world. At eight, she was painted by masters, caught in photographs, shown to advantage in moving pictures. Yet by the age of nine, her fame had vanished. No one spoke of her or knew her name. And why? One day, she had fallen in love with the simplest of dives, the pin-drop. She refused to do any other, and so all her planned exhibitions were out of the question. Any child can do a pin-drop. She returned to the town of her birth and, abandoned by her managers and various hangers on, made as though to continue her life.

—Will you go first, or shall I? asked Linus.

—I shall, said Vera, and cast herself off the cliff in a perfect shining arc.

Vera and Linus came one day to a vacant farm in the country.

They went inside immediately. There was a big kitchen, three empty rooms, and opposite to the front door there were stairs down to some floor beneath.

Vera and Linus descended.

On the stairs they felt a grasping fear and thought of going back. But their feet led them down.

—No one is here beside ourselves, they did not say, and looked desperately into each other's eyes.

They emerged into a large gloomy place floored with wood. In the middle was a chair and on the floor about it, four filthy gloves. In the corner they saw a little table and on it a tiny guttering candle.

—It seems someone has been here already, said Vera nervously.

—But now we are here, said Linus, holding tight her hand.

—Here and nowhere else.

Vera assembled all the leaders of the country in her drawing room and menaced them all with lions and such, saying, let this be a lesson to you, and also, you shall not leave this house alive.

Linus was abed.

—I am cold and cannot sleep, he said.

Vera wrapped herself about him and tried to make him warm, but Linus persisted in shivering.

So Vera wove a little wool-blanket for Linus that she put over him.
This did not help.

So Vera cut off her hair and wove it into the blanket along with the heat of her blood and the warmth of her breath.

This blanket she laid over Linus.

—Now you can sleep, she said feeling herself lessen and dissolve.

But Linus was far away.

Vera and Linus found a little bird whose beak had been broken.

—Poor little bird, said Linus. Who did this to you?

—The little boy who destroys everything he sees with his hammer, murmured the bird.

—Poor little bird. What can we do for you?

—I have an idea, said Vera. Perhaps it can live in the forest as a tree.

—Let's see.

So Vera and Linus took the bird into the forest where it changed into a tree. And happily it throve.

But in a few days, the little boy was found hanging by a thin swollen neck, his front teeth shattered by his own hammer.

The townspeople sought vengefully for those who had hanged him, but all in vain.

A week after his death a place was made for the boy beneath a pile of faded leaves near to where the woods begin.

I wrought a morning from green bottle glass and sang it to sleep in the gentle sunlight. The wilds began at land's edge, where the water used to be. And what a land for a young man! A land full of deeds and sure-footed travels, cardinal dangers. But I was so old then, I could barely lift a soup-spoon.

The woman who came occasionally to feed me wore moccasins and I was plagued by her sudden arrivals. Are there to be no secrets? I cried.

And then, children ran by. Myself, at the ages of six, eight and ten.

—I'll come with you! I cried, and when I woke all this was just beginning.

Vera came home with a thing that she locked inside a small chest.

—What is the secret? asked Linus, excited.

—I cannot tell you, Vera said. And you may not peek. Absolutely NOT!

Days passed and Linus continuously thought of what the secret could be. He could not stop thinking about it no matter how he tried. But Vera refused to speak of it. Whenever Linus mentioned it, her manner changed and she would ignore him.

Eventually Linus could stand it no longer. When Vera was away, he opened the chest.

But at that moment, the image of his Vera started to fade in his mind, more and more.

Until she transformed into the wind.
And the wind.

# A Lesson in Dreams

Devices to be employed while traveling in sleep. Gestures of the hand, memorized cants, ideas of light, circular steps and methods of backtracking. The primary skill of dreams is that of ambuscade. A man named Drago Pentacost, finding himself alive in the twelfth century, was undoubtedly the greatest dreamer in recorded history. His manual, Psyche and Tools of Water, was only made in six copies, all of which were destroyed by the church, yet tales of his deeds can be found in church archives and relate to us a genius such as has seldom been equaled. It is said in dreams that one may request of someone a service and, if the request is stated properly, one may not be refused. Thus Pentacost built his home with the aid of crickets and weasels. He set a guard over himself by day with the aid of clouds. His way through thick fields was made easy by the bending of grass, the beckoning of wind. Indeed, he is said never to have walked up a hill, so kind was the ground to his passing. He made a compact in his last days and found a place in a deep turn where rows of trees made increased of morning. Is it known to you? For many have lost their way in this guess, that the shape of the land and light can make doors in the mind. Faring now on a ship out of storms and Zanzibar, I carve a figure out of bone, a man in a cloak. Of course, there is a compartment hidden beneath the cloak, and in it a slip of paper naming my successor. On a day like this anyone may be found or lost. Things happen with such ease I can't describe.

Vera and Linus were walking along a promenade when Linus gestured wildly at a girl who was walking a short distance ahead of them.

—There we are! he shouted.

—How can that be? But you are right, said Vera. It is we.

—Let's follow after, said Linus.

And so they did.

They followed the girl all the while debating how it could be that a girl might walk the streets unaware that she is not one but two.

—But possibly she knows, said Vera. Or has sensed it.

—I doubt that, said Linus. I doubt that.

—But we shall make her become aware of it.

—Indeed.

Vera found a man who knew the TELLING VOICE and she studied under him for 9 years, living with him in his stinking shack beside a filth-ridden river. Nine years and a day gathered all in a tawdry cloth and kept like a calendar.

One day she returned.

The forest was the same as before. Linus was standing out in his shirt sleeves chopping what at first appeared to be wood but on closer inspection proved to be the hardy reputations of many famous men. He looked fondly on her.

—My Vera, he said. How far you have been! How needlessly long!

—Run about like a stoat, said Vera in the telling voice.

And Linus had no choice. All that day he ran about in the yard like a stoat while Vera moved about in the house, putting things to right and pleasing herself with this thought or that.

Vera and Linus retained possession of the child's heart which Vera had once cut from a little boy. They had maintained it at a proper temperature, and tended to it well.

But one day Linus got the idea that they should plant the heart. Vera concurred.

They fetched a flowerpot and put mould in the bottom. There on top they laid the heart, filled up the pot and pressed carefully down with their hands. Then they waited curiously to see what would happen.

Days passed and weeks. And in the end of the second month, a little sprout peeked up from the mould.

Vera and Linus nearly burst with joy.

—We must name it, said Vera.

Linus betook himself to thought and then proposed that its name was Hanúk.

—He grows fast when he is spoken to and shown attention, but fades rapidly under neglect. He likes beautiful music but hates loud noise, and is sensitive to overmuch sunshine or heat. How much he likes the dusk!

Vera contemplated the plant and petted its tiny leaves that were starting to appear even as they spoke.

—Hello, my friend, she said.

And then she sang the plant Hanúk a song about the moon.

Vera and Linus pretended that they were forced to say goodbye.

They embraced each other as hard as they could and whispered parting words in each other's ear.

And Vera began to cry.

Linus held her tightly saying that which might console her.

—Don't cry my love. We don't have to say goodbye. Perhaps later. Perhaps one day, later. But not now.

He said this, and also,

—But even if it will happen one day, we are only practicing now. Nothing more. This is a rehearsal, a rehearsal, my love.

—Imagine that we are two leaves on a big tree, said Linus

and blew the last drops from Vera's eyes.

—Vera, said Linus one day. Why not be a forest and stand in solemnity for all of time?

And so Vera stood like a forest. All around her there grew up a massive quiet. Birds learned of her sanctuary and fled to her in the long evenings. Burrows formed in the places between her roots. Lone bees buzzed in the glassy enclaves of shorn light.

—As agreed then, said Linus.

—As agreed, said the shipwrights.

And the shipwrights came out of hiding and took saws and axes and cut Vera down and cut Vera up and made of the forest of Vera nineteen ships with which to sail the high seas.

The window was open and in the sink a little paper-boat was sailing.

(On which a message was written for Vera). She took it from the water and read:

—When there appears a cloud on the sky in the shape of a tree, you shall walk two steps backwards, then close your eyes and count to ten. Then you can begin again.

Linus composed a book about a man who could set forth beyond his body at night to cause trouble in the town for those he disliked.

—Was it his shadow that went forth? asked Vera. Was it his soul?

—No, said Linus. It was more like this …

and he went forth then and there from himself and Vera followed after some ways until she lost him at a crossroads and stood there some while in thought unwilling to turn back.

—What mischief will he do? she said aloud.

And you and I would do well to wonder the same.

Vera and Linus had a wager. The loser would walk the streets of their town with an open jar of salt and strew it in keeping with the victor's will.

Vera lost the wager.

Linus brought her an expensive jar of salt and out they went. He picked a good spot in the town center occluded behind a wall,

—This is where you'll start, he said.

Then he conducted her here and there.

But when they had reached the other end of the center and the salt was nearly finished, Linus bade her stop.

—Make a circle of salt, he said.

Vera did so. She knelt and spun smoothly and slowly so there formed a distinct line of white.

Then she stood, awaiting in the circle Linus's company.

Vera and Linus built a little window for themselves. Inside the window two children, a boy and a girl, were fighting over a ball. They snatched it from each other growing more and more angry until they fell to fighting. They kicked and yelled, pulled each other's hair, and wept while trying to get the ball from each other.

—On whose side are you? asked Linus.

Vera thought for a second. But at that moment the ball escaped from the children and rolled towards the window. And Vera and Linus saw that it wasn't a ball after all, but the head of a third child who seemed to have been a girl.

Linus found a shallow hole in the ground.

He set himself to digging deeper with his hands and so he did until he felt something hard as of metal. He dug around it and brought it up into the day.

Opening it, Linus was astonished when he saw that it was full of small things that had been dear to himself in his childhood.

But one strange thing there was: the object — that which had been dearest was gone missing.

Vera and Linus set out to construct an atlas of nightmares. They bought a great bolt of yellow cloth and they spread it out across their good names.

—Here, they said, we shall honestly abide.

First Linus brought in a woman he had seen through a window years before.

—Lie upon that sheet, he said, and die.

So commissioned, she did so.

Then Vera brought a town abandoned by a broken mill.

—Go there, she said, and sleep.

At her command, the town reclined and soon was senseless.

Oh the many and varied things they brought! Contentious elephants, poisonous flowers, flights of insects, passages from cruel letters.

Finally they built a wall of stone about the place with a great stone arch and they took to chasing men and women, children, animals, all beneath the arch.

Not a one did ever return.

Vera and Linus attacked a bicyclist and threw him down in the street in the aim of fulfilling Linus's long desired wish.

The man tumbled down to the pavement and lost consciousness. Blood streamed from a big cut on his head. His countenance, though, was peaceful and Vera and Linus pondered whether he was dead.

—I like him, said Linus.

—Yes, he's nice, Vera agreed.

And she dipped her finger in the warm bloodstream that made its way through the street.

Vera painted wrinkles on herself and pretended to be an old lady. She dyed her hair grey and walked around limping.

—My Vera. What happened to you? asked Linus quite shocked.

But Vera did not explain.

And before the day had ended Linus himself had aged past mending.

Vera and Linus found a tiny door in the corner of a shop they had gone to once. They found the door while remembering after many years, though of course, by then, it had long since closed.

—Shall we go through? asked Linus.

And then they were through. There was a sort of alcove such as one would find in a library, and then there was the library itself, grand and stretching in every direction thousands and thousands of shelves and beyond shelves corridors presided over by stained glass and crowning rotundas.

Many people were there, walking, reading, consulting, sitting in whispering dialogue.

—I am afraid, said Vera, that we are too young yet to understand any book we might find here.

For indeed, Vera and Linus suddenly seemed very young, much too young to be of any use at all.

So they played beneath the tables and in the long halls many games of their own contriving and when the day ended they were caught and taken out into the night where this account may not follow.

Vera and Linus wondered whether a plant that grew from and was fed by a human heart would differ from all other plants.

—It must be, said Vera.

—Perhaps it will have as many senses as we, hidden in the recesses of stalks and leaves, said Linus.

—...So it might see us! said Vera gleefully.

—Or it could bear untoward fruit that has never been seen before, said Linus.

—And inside every one there would be nerves and blood.

—Or perhaps a human tooth.

Vera and Linus up to a mountain in the roasting sun. Their shadows were tiny, lost things, and the earth under their feet was bone-dry.

Near the mountaintop they met a woman who lived there in a little hut. She drew water in a glass bottle that she gave them to drink by the door.

But when Vera and Linus had slaked their thirst, a deep voice burst from inside the hut. The woman responded nervously and in haste, saying that she must certainly close the door but that Vera and Linus could wait for her outside until she returned.

They decided to wait. But a long wait it was, all through the hot day; and at night she came.

Linus wrote a letter to Vera one night while she slept. It was three hundred pages long and when he finished, his hand would not work for two days and a night.

What could such a letter contain?

A catalog of angers.

In it, Linus described anger in all its varieties, forgetting none. He wrote out passages illustrating each kind, and painted in blood and watercolors details in the margin.

Linus came to Vera with something hidden between his hands.

—What do you have? asked Vera.

—Never can you guess.

—Is it a stone? she said. A rat ... or a baby?

—None of these, said Linus.

And he opened his palms to reveal a tiny eyeless bird ringed by cats.

At the beginning, he wrote out each version of the anger, numbering them all. Each kind of each version, each category, each subcategory: none escaped his nimble hand. This led to equations of anger, a mathematics of symptoms and causes.

Vera read it in the morning light. She read aloud:

And the fury of the sea is not constant, for when it is seen by a young wife on a road above the water it is one thing, but when seen by an aging captain who may surround it with a thousand ships and days it is another. When it is seen from a shallow boat, when it is seen from a proud frigate, when it is peered at through a glass jar in a pantry, noted in a dark engraving in the smoke of an inn, or come upon after great distance, as in passage from the moon light travels in a duller coat, as if to disguise itself and speaks only words it has heard in the pastures of morning.

Ah, the pastures of morning, where one waited so long as a child.

What is to become of my few and many selves?

Linus sat by the window and saw an old bearded man appear with a voluminous black bag over his shoulder. The man passed the window once but then turned back.

He walked back and forth many times and finally halted right before the window, facing Linus.

Then they looked each other in the eye.

1. Linus made an enemy of a powerful man.

2. This man considered the matter of Linus, sitting in an immense rosewood chamber surrounded by cronies and attendants, themselves powerful men in their own right.

3. He sent to the government, mouth-organ that rests ever in the pocket of the wealthy, and the matter was laid before a secret committee. What was to be done?

4. —We shall have Linus murdered, they said, one to another, and sent for two operatives. The first would find the place where Linus was living, and operate the motorcar. The second would approach Linus and kill him with gunfire.

5. HOW DID EVENTS UNFOLD?

6. The first found Linus where he was living on an old property of stone and orchards by the sounding sea. He was observed in his machinations, though he knew it not, and he went away to fetch the second man.

7. The first and second men returned to the house of Linus by car. The first waited with great poise and daring by the roadside with the engine purring.

8. The second stepped onto Linus's land.

9. We wait inside the house, all of us, and when we see the man approaching across the lawn, we giggle and finger our nets and knives. He comes to the door, uses fancy tools to break the lock and enters.

10. Then we catch him in a net, take his gun, break it with a hammer, remove all his clothes and confine him, like a dress-form, to an old dusty room.

11. The man with the motorcar we gas and drop into the sea.

12. THEN: over a period of days we draw out of the man all the details of the planned assassination. We do this with kind persuasion and rewards of treacle, toast and tea. Also, we demonstrate our knowledge of the agent's real life by showing him photographs of his family, etc, in their home, en route to and from school, etc. Soon we have all the details of the plot.

13. Next we set up a film camera in the courtyard. We film the agent as he explains to the camera everything he's told us.

14. He says as well that he has been properly fed and not drugged or dealt with unkindly.

15. —I am an assassin, he says, in the pay of the national government. I was sent to kill an innocent man.

and also

—Please, think well of me.

16. Then the man is given a knife, and Linus is given a knife, and the film crew shoots a moving picture.

17. The man cuts Linus in the arm. He cuts Linus in the face. He is really quite good with a knife.

18. Then, Linus puts the knife into the man's lung and moves it around quite a bit before removing it. The man lies down on the ground and drops his own knife.

19. Next, we put the man into a box and send him in great ceremony and kindness to his widow and family.

20. In great gladness and with indignant manner, we cause the film to be shown throughout the nation. This is embarrassing for many people who believed the nation to be a kindly functioning democracy.

21. YET Linus is hounded by the police and forced to leave the country, charged with the murder of both men.

22. YET THIS:

One day, the powerful man, who is spoken of in 1. and 2. sits down to breakfast in his fine style of living. However the room is quieter than ever before. In fact, Linus is sitting beside him.

—Good day, says Linus.

Before the man can speak, he is bound and gagged. Then, an operation is performed on him to insert a small charge of dynamite into the space beside the man's shriveled heart. A radio-receiver is attached.

23. —From now on, says Linus, I will send you instructions each Tuesday in a blue envelope. You shall never again have a will of your own. If someone were to describe you in the years to come as having spent the latter part of your life as a toy in the hands of a

hostile power, that description could not easily be dismissed.

Vera and Linus found a blind girl upon a bench.

They walked up to her and invited her to come with them, and she accepted, offering them each a hand.

Vera and Linus led her through the streets, describing everything they saw, trees, houses and laughing children at play with stones.

—And here is a high and large iron-fence, said Vera. But what is behind it we shall not tell you … though soon you will find out.

Linus woke up in the middle of the night. He felt sick and went to get a glass of water, the which he drank all at once. But when he put the glass away he heard a strange noise coming from outside. He looked out the window but outdoors the sun wasn't so he didn't see a thing.

Linus got dressed and put on coat and shoes. The noise stopped just as he was ready, but he went out anyway to reconnoiter.

In the dim dark he saw someone standing. He approached this person and when he got closer he found that the person resembled himself and was peering back at him.

—Who are you? Linus asked, concerned.

The other one said nothing, only kept on looking at him with a straight face. Then Linus saw the man's outlines become fainter until he dissolved and was gone.

Linus stood still for a while staring at the spot where the man had been, both astonished and frightened, then returned to the house perturbed.

When back inside, the noises recommenced.

Linus hurried into the bedroom and woke Vera so she could see. But she only murmured something from her slumber and was not to be woken.

—Do you not hear this? asked Linus.

But Vera was fast asleep.

Linus lay down beside her and stared up at the ceiling unsure whether he should venture out again.

Vera dug a hole in the garden. Then she covered over the top with a blanket and covered the blanket in leaves and the vestiges of last year's garden.

—Who, I wonder, said she, will come walking and end up in that hole?

She placed a boat hook and a picked lilac on the far side.

—Someone must see the lilac, someone must see the boat hook, someone must see these things and come to fetch them, she said.

Oh how fine a day that will be!

Vera sat in the kitchen where she was boiling water for tea. When it was ready she poured it over the leaves in the cup and added a spoon of honey.

But as soon the first sip passed her lips she heard a voice speaking.

—Is there none for me?

—What …?

Vera looked around in surprise. The voice was low and rough, and Vera could by no means find where it came from.

—Do I get nothing?

—What do you mean?

—Others are thirsty besides you.

—Thirsty for tea …? said Vera.

—Well, I would prefer the very coldest water.

—Yes, certainly. I have the juice of oranges as well. Would you rather that?

—NO, absolutely not!! I'm not even sure it's good for me.

—Why would it not be good for you? Vera asked surprised.

—Well, I'm not used to it. You always give me cold

water from the sink. But not lately. I haven't gotten a single drop this whole week.

Now Vera suddenly understood what was going on and who it was talking. It was none other than Hanúk, the little tree that she and Linus had grown in the kitchen window.

—Oh, it's YOU! she trumpeted. Oh, I am sorry that we forgot you these many days. I am SO sorry, I promise you it will never happen again. Never, never!

—Uhh …

—Can you forgive us, dear friend?

—I suppose.

Vera watered this Hanúk of theirs, and with the watering came happy-noises.

But with the passing of his thirst, he grew silent, just as silent as he'd been before.

## DO YOU REMEMBER THE CHILD BURIED IN THE FIELD?

Vera and Linus went sometimes to visit it. Was there anything so joyous, so grand, so redolent of spring and the world's new incarnation than to grip the still vivacious hand of a long buried child?

—We must have a festival, said Linus.

And so they called upon all those who played instruments and upon all who would dance and sing and they had a glad festival, a FESTIVAL

of the   STILL   MOVING   HAND!

Yet there were some who stood apart and thought ill of them for this.

Vera and Linus wanted to procure a friend who was a runner of great distances in the day and night so they went hunting in suitable distance.

Most people they saw were without conceivable merit; they were by no means worthy of knowing such as Vera and Linus.

But eventually they saw one who stood head and shoulders above the rest.

This woman shone like a mirror in finely tailored clothing beyond description and ran with a gallop that pleased them to no end.

So Vera and Linus decided that she and no other should be their new friend.

They consulted one another and plotted furiously, and as they drew deeper into their conceits, Vera grew concerned.

—We must though take care to have her around only when we should want a friend like that, she said.

—Certainly we will not want that very often, Linus said. But once in a while, don't you think?

—Yes. I do think so, said Vera. But only once in a while.

Vera drew a map of the death of honor in the modern world.

—There is no honor left, she said.

Linus came down from a wooden platform and lay in the grass at her side.

—Can there be justice without honor? he asked.

—Only the punishment of children, said Vera, by other children.

Linus tore the legs off an ant and grafted in their place the long bodies of six caterpillars.

This new creature writhed and rippled.

—If I were to say beneath the ground the king grows, awaiting his return, what could that possibly mean? asked Vera.

—We shall raise this fellow as our own, declared Linus, lifting up the ant.

—We shall read him URN BURIAL and also THE RIDDLE OF THE SANDS. His first words will be, I wake from a dream with a thorn in my cheek.

But already the ant was dead.

Linus stood by the riverbank.

He stared at the box in his hands that contained what should never be forgotten.

But something else though was gone into the river.

Vera found a little box in the grass containing a door knob amongst much broken glass.

—This will do well for Linus, she said.

And in the evening she gave it to him along with a little poem about the sun.

Vera decided to hide from Linus by pretending to be a wall in the room where Linus was sitting in a chair by the fire with a cup of tea.

Linus knew Vera was there though he pretended not to notice.

He finished his tea and then sought a deck of cards and began the solitaire called never never.

Vera did not know that her hiding place was known to the one from whom she hid, and this was fortunate, for how sad she would have been!

She remained the wall for hours while Linus played without victory, the game called never never,

over and again by the fire.

Vera decided to set a riddle-path. She crept from bed early and set up a camera to take many pictures in a row.

1. She photographed herself sneaking out of bed.

2. She photographed herself leaving the house.

3. She photographed herself making her way across the lawn to a secret hiding place beneath the brambles of the fence.

4. Then she came out from beneath the fence, removed the film from the camera, printed it, and constructed a flip-book using the many pictures of her passage.

She stood proudly holding the flip book. She ran her thumb over the pages and watched herself rise from bed and move in stilted fashion out of the house, across the lawn, into the distance beneath the brambles.

This book she laid in her place beside Linus in the bed.

Then away again into hiding.

—This, Vera confided to the fence post, is the life I have chosen from many.

Vera and Linus arrived on a deserted island.

There were many seas,
smooth and fair-blue, rough and grey.

There were many skies,
sunny and bright,
wreathed in red and violet,
or heavily overwhelmed in grey.

And time passed.

The sun set and rose again. That's just how it happened, day after day.

Vera and Linus didn't know how long they had been on the island for time stretched unknown in all directions meanwhile refusing to exist in any actual form.

They looked about for a ship in what they might call an hour or a day and had nearly lost all hope of it going to happen.

But some mornings yet there came a shouting:

—THERE'S A SHIP!

Linus, pointing out to the ocean. And this he did just for the pleasure of it, even though it was perhaps never to be true.

Linus bought a skin-drum and took to pounding it on the rooftops of a morning.

—I shall call the insects, the animals to war.

And when he beat his drum the insects gathered, rising in clans and concatenations.

The birds became aware of this, both slowly and all at once, as is their way, and soon the sky was filled.

Birds eating insects. Insects falling in common upon birds. Small rats and mice darting through the madcap crowd.

And all the while the pounding of the drum.

Linus did a little trick on Vera,
causing all her fingers to disappear.

—Shall they come back? said Vera,
worry in her voice.

—I'm sure they may, said Linus narrowing his eyes,
already inventing his next trick.

Vera and Linus went to someone's country-house where a shooting party was on.

—I am an expert shot, said Vera.

—At least, I have dreamed it, said Linus.

And all day the pheasants flew up away into the sky, driven by the beaters, and all day they were brought down again by the line of shooters.

Vera held the shotguns and reloaded for Linus in the manner of a trusted servant.

Linus held the shotguns and reloaded for Vera in the manner of a trusted servant.

—I believe we should eat all that we shoot, said Vera.

—I believe we should eat all that we shoot, said Linus, both humans and animals.

So they made a heavily spiced but honeyed and delicate partridge stew and served it with hot buttermilk scones and lemonade.

—What will we kill next? they wondered quietly, with sauce-spattered mouths and dirty hands.

Linus heard a strange noise inside the bathroom
and went to find it.

Within there was no one.

But in the mirror he saw a face
that sometimes came to him at night.

In the house there lived a woman who kept herself completely apart from the others. She was careful to never open the door if someone was near, and from her rooms came an unfortunate smell that woke the suspicions of Vera and Linus.

—I am sure that she is hiding something, said Vera.

—You are right, said Linus. And what it is we shall find out.


They left a little wooden bird sitting on a branch where he could see directly to the woman's door. Then they went away.

Two days later Vera and Linus returned to get the bird and ask him for news.

—Did you manage to see inside? Linus asked excited.

—Yes, I certainly did, said the bird full of pride.

—And what did you see! What did you see!

The bird fluffed up his feathers and puffed out his chest.

—She took out the garbage yesterday and I saw straight in. Who but I could see she had an egg on the floor on a sheepskin?

He paused for a second.

—But this was no regular egg. It was prodigious. Like an ostrich-egg. Yes, bigger than that.

Vera and Linus gasped and grinned.

—An egg!

—We must get it away from her, said Linus.

—But what could be inside it? asked Vera.

—It could be anything. Likely, a mammal.

—Or a monster, said Vera.

—Or even a human, said the bird.

—But whatever it is, we must find out, said Linus doggedly.

—And we shall find out by making it ours.

Vera and Linus lay in bed during the cold months and refused to come out from beneath the covers. Their little house was tucked up in the snow and a little fire burned in the stove. The windows all were frosted over and icicles hung from the eves.

It was at such times that their great learning began, for their bed was surrounded entirely by piles of books which they would read both alone and together.

Sometimes they would send to the kitchen for something nice to eat, or something hot to drink.

They corresponded with the outer world by carrier pigeon.

How Linus loved to make the little messages and tie them to the birds' legs!

But of course, this is a lie. There are no more such pigeons. Even the quietest dismalest schoolboy knows that.

No, they used a telegraph and morse code. Sometimes the tapping and clicking would fill the afternoon and spill over into the evening leaving the house so startled that it rose up like a wounded archer beneath the hooves of a cavalry charge.

What furious messages they sent, I can't begin to tell you.

Linus was given two mice of which he became quite fond.

Even too fond, thought Vera.

So once when Linus was away, she broke both their necks and took them outside in her pocket. Then she threw them into an open window in the street.

Yet afterwards she felt bad about the whole thing, so she caught new mice in the woods for Linus before returning home.

Linus showed some doubts about his mice as soon as he laid eyes on them.

—These are not mine … he said. Can it be?!

And he looked at Vera with a grave suspicion.

She looked away.

—Vera! Where are my mice? he asked.

—What did you do to them?

She kept silent for a while not looking at Linus.

But soon enough she admitted everything.

—Did you really kill them?! That's awful, he said.

—My dearest little ones, he added sadly. How much I loved them.

But with these words Vera's anger was woken again.

—Yes. And afterwards I threw them into the neighbors' window, she said. It is true and I hope you will never forgive me.

Vera and Linus went about in a dense place of trees. Thereafter they came to a flatness with great length of sky.

A girl was there pretending to be a bird, or a bird a girl.

In the sky was a cloud shaped like the grasping maw of a wolf.

Over many countries, said the bird, there are clouds like wolves, telling people that someone has just now been eaten by a wolf.

The girl nodded, and a cloud passed over her small face. But of it she said nothing.

Vera came to, motionless,
wrapped in the thickest of blankets.

But when they covered her face
she felt how the cold overtook her.

Linus had a silent week.

On the sixth day Vera was fed up with having no one to speak with.

So Linus decided to bring her company.

The door opened into the room where Vera was sitting in chair. In came half a person, with a body from foot to waist.

Vera burst out laughing.

—I shall at least need the rest of him if we are to speak, she said.

In came the rest, sailing in the air and singing, and strangely enough, the voice could have been Linus's.

And all at once it seemed a whole year had gone round and it was time once again for the making of the doll-baron, the sending of the doll-baron down the river to the king in the depths of the sea.

—As in years past, said Linus, we shall cast sorrow away.

So they sat cross-legged like tailors do and they stitched and cut and stitched. After great labor, the doll lay finished, finely stuffed and rounded with a light green jacket, yellow trousers, a garish red face and a little blue cap such as might be found deep in your pleasure. He wore no shoes for it was his duty to go barefoot in others' troubles.

And all at once it seemed the time for confiding had arrived. Vera went first, taking the doll with her to a bend in the hallway. There they sat and she related all her worries, displeasures, ill-fates. The baron-doll said scarcely a word, but it quite seemed as though it had heard.

Then Linus took the doll to the roof and they sat westward watching while Linus sang a song about his troubles. It was sung in the old manner, rather more a list than a song, and soon it was finished, though after quite a while, I should think, if the truth be told.

Then down with the doll together to the river where they built with intricate skill and infinite delicacy a basket of reeds and sticks. In they put the doll and they turned his face away, saying

—Such as he is really to be pitied,

and also

—Will they be kind to him at the bottom of the sea?

And with a gentle push he was out in the current and, as it was said many times long ago, though little now, their sorrows were carried away by this messenger to the court of the sea-king, and dined on there to much acclaim, kept there like a fashionable season.

Vera approached Linus with a little stone.

—Where can we put it? she asked.

Linus slid a knife out of his sleeve and cut a hole in the trunk of a large tree.

—It fits perfectly, he said.

—It fits perfectly ... like an eye.

Vera and Linus went walking in the middle night.

—We shall go to the lighthouse that stands in a great darkness out at land's end, they said.

So they walked for a time and passed beyond all the street lamps until it was dark all around them and they could find their way only by the noise of the sea on their left and the pin of the lighthouse lit in the uncertain distance.

On they went, and soon a storm rose up.

Wind blew, rain poured sideways with great width and power.

Linus felt a strange reluctance to continue. He stopped, and Vera went on, pulling on his arm. They walked a few steps. Then Linus stopped again.

The storm rose up then in truth, untying the bags in which all four winds are kept. In moments Vera and Linus were soaked to the skin.

—You must turn back, said the storm.

—For we can go no further, said Vera.

—For we can go no further, said Linus.

and also

—Something was waiting at the lighthouse. The weather knew, and came to stand between and see we wouldn't come to harm.

Linus was alone in the room drinking his tea
and reading a book that delighted him.

And this was nice.

But it still made him feel sad
to look up
and see Vera's absence in the wall.

Vera and Linus had marionettes cut in the shape of themselves.

And in the evenings Linus danced for Vera in a beautiful custom as of old
while Vera sang with her eyes half closed,
holding a card between her hands let drop to the floor

with no sound

just before the curtain fell.

With what book can you reckon death? With an old book? With a bible? With a book bound in the skin of a priest? For there are such books, but they cannot be found easily, and the cost is much, perhaps more than you can pay.

Linus lifted his heart in the midst of a crimson pond. This is the last time we will see each other, he thought, and then the rowboat was abreast of him, and Vera was there, and he climbed up and in.

—You were too long in the wilds, my love, said Vera. For look now, even the hairs of your face and head have grown long.

—Yet my eyes are thin and small, said Linus. And I drape over the same bones.

Then the sky was filled with kites that rustled with the uncertainty of war.

Has the time at last come upon us? they cried, but no sound came. For even then the world was being folded up in immense sheets of paper. Six men came along a crease, wearing the heads of frogs, laden down with an enormous burden.

—We shall help you! cried Vera, abandoning the boat.

But the burden was only enough for the frog-men, and when it was threatened, they disappeared.

Where they had been there was only the sound of pages being turned deep within a house.

—Such has always been my inheritance, said Linus.

And they walked hand in hand to where no fate would spare them.

# END

0.14.1

# NOTES to the TEXT

### 1.

This work was composed during the winter and early spring of 2006 in Montpellier, France.

During that time, we lived at 23, Rue de l'Amandier, in the old section, beside the Iglise St. Anne.

### 2.

Alda Ægisdottir, both bird and girl, must be credited with having invented the riddle from 2.29.1, and also the cloud-observation from 2.29.2.

### 3.

We would like to thank the good people at Nyhil for doing everything in their power to ensure that this book would be a fine pocket edition.

### 4.

The frontispiece still was shot by Catherine Despont on Île d'Yeu, 23 January 2006.

### 5.

0 and 3 are additional designations, the first for early and late material, the second for drawings.

6.

The font employed throughout is Cochin.

7.

EXPLANATION OF DRAWINGS

in the case of misunderstanding.

3.1.1 is Vera with a parasol.
3.1.2 is a *fox* in a suit of human skin.
3.1.3 is the same, seen from behind.
3.1.4 is a girl in a bird suit.
3.1.5 is an overlarge duck in the drawing style of C. Ball.
3.1.6 is a girl with own head.
3.1.7 is the king of the cat o' nine tails. WMJJR.

8.

Translation: All texts marked 1.x.x have been translated from the Icelandic by the committee of Jesse Ball and Thordis Björnsdottir.

9.

Acknowledgement to: Publishing Editor Vidar Thorsteinsson and Quaestor Thor Steinarsson of Nyhil, and to Catherine Ball, archivist of Smithtown Library.

# INDEX OF FIRST LINES
alphabetical

| | |
|---|---|
| A big black cat was sitting in the windowsill ... | 1.20.1 |
| A bird that Vera caught and tied to her ankle .... | 2.18.1 |
| A day and a day and a day ... | 2.7.2 |
| A highwayman must carry a weapon ... | 2.25.2 |
| A highwayman must know the land ... | 2.25.1 |
| A lesson in dreams | 2.37.1 |
| A waylayer must dress well ... | 2.25.5 |
| Act to ruin other routs ... | 2.25.22 |
| An old man sat on a chair in the corner ... | 1.7.1 |
| And all at once it seemed ... | 2.48.1 |
| And indeed for such as we ... | 2.25.7 |
| And Linus betook himself ... | 2.25.0 |
| And out went Vera and Linus with a large knife ... | 1.25.1 |
| And Varsithon ... | 2.22.2 |
| And withal they dreamed first ... | 2.10.1 |
| Any plot hatched in the town ... | 2.25.18 |
| Assign to yourself some. | 2.25.23 |
| At the beginning he wrote out ... | 2.43.2 |
| Be of good cheer ... | 2.25.26 |
| Be of good fortune in word and deed ... | 2.25.16 |
| Consider the wife, the husband ... | 2.25.14 |
| Do you remember the child ... | 2.6.4 |
| Exchange your take ... | 2.25.25 |
| For though the moon is not a river ... | 2.23.2 |
| Has the time at last come ... | 2.51.1 |
| Have it known that you yourself ... | 2.25.15 |
| I would very much like ... | 1.23.1 |
| I wrought a morning ... | 2.36.1 |
| If a dog were to learn to speak ... | 2.33.1 |
| If you do not wish to cultivate ... | 2.25.20 |
| Imagine that we are two leaves ... | 1.43.2 |

| | |
|---|---|
| In a small house there lived an old man … | 1.17.1 |
| In the event of capture … | 2.25.12 |
| In the house there lived a woman … | 1.61.1 |
| In the night Vera cut off all of Linus's hair. | 2.3.1 |
| In the person of your known name … | 2.25.13 |
| In your approach to a stopped carriage … | 2.25.17 |
| It was night and the weather held still … | 1.28.3 |
| Keep a memory of all places … | 2.25.11 |
| Keep a record of all your waylayings … | 2.25.27 |
| Let us go, said Vera to Linus, to picnic … | 2.6.2 |
| Let's go for a walk, said Linus. | 1.13.1 |
| Linus bought a skin-drum … | 2.45.4 |
| Linus bound his method … | 2.25.28 |
| Linus broke a bottle on the floor … | 1.9.1 |
| Linus came to Vera with … | 1.51.1 |
| Linus came to Vera with a tiny … | 1.29.1 |
| Linus came upon a girl and a bird … | 2.29.1 |
| Linus composed a book … | 2.40.1 |
| Linus crawled up from the earth … | 1.19.1 |
| Linus crept out in the night to go and see … | 1.23.1 |
| Linus did a little trick on Vera … | 1.60.1 |
| Linus discovered one day a little book … | 2.16.1 |
| Linus found a girl who was but an inch tall. | 2.32.1 |
| Linus found a hole in between … | 1.16.1 |
| Linus found a page … | 2.23.3 |
| Linus found a shallow hole … | 1.47.1 |
| Linus gave Vera a blue glass-bird. | 1.31.1 |
| Linus had a silent week. | 1.64.1 |
| Linus had made a dress for Vera. | 1.1.1 |
| Linus heard a strange noise … | 1.54.2 |
| Linus kissed Vera … | 2.11.1 |
| Linus looks up from his lifetime of … | 2.19.1 |
| Linus made an enemy of a powerful man … | 2.44.1 |
| Linus picked Vera up … | 2.17.1 |
| Linus reached under Vera's dress … | 2.26.9 |

| | |
|---|---|
| Linus sat by the window ... | 1.52.1 |
| Linus stood by the riverbank ... | 1.56.1 |
| Linus surprised Vera in her bath. | 2.9.1 |
| Learn to speak the dialects ... | 2.25.21 |
| Linus was abed. | 1.39.1 |
| Linus was alone ... | 1.58.2 |
| Linus was given two mice ... | 1.62.1 |
| Linus was once walking alone in the forest ... | 1.28.1 |
| Linus was sleeping. Vera wanted ... | 2.4.1 |
| Linus went to a little field ... | 2.28.1 |
| Linus went to the chest in the room ... | 2.2.1 |
| Linus woke up in the middle of the night ... | 1.54.1 |
| Linus wrote a letter to Vera ... | 2.43.1 |
| Never show mercy once your intent ... | 2.25.24 |
| No. 32 | 2.6.3 |
| On the seventh day ... | 1.36.1 |
| One must speak clearly and well ... | 2.25.19 |
| Said Linus ... | 2.14.1 |
| Shall we speak of the frequency of attacks ... | 2.25.10 |
| The dark parade now and then ... | 2.24.1 |
| The effect on one's reputation ... | 2.25.4 |
| The highwayman must have a servant ... | 2.25.8 |
| The servant's ties to the near town ... | 2.25.9 |
| The sun set and rose ... | 1.59.2 |
| The waylayer must have in his keeping ... | 2.25.6 |
| The Willow Path | 2.5.1 |
| The window was open and in the sink ... | 1.44.1 |
| They all stood silently in a line ... | 1.4.1 |
| They were out walking in evening ... | 1.21.1 |
| This day it was pouring rain ... | 1.18.1 |
| To speak of the last made thought ... | 2.25.3 |
| Vera and Linus attacked a bicyclist ... | 1.48.1 |
| Vera and Linus built a little window ... | 1.46.1 |
| Vera and Linus came one day to a vacant ... | 1.38.1 |
| Vera and Linus came upon a winged creature ... | 1.33.1 |

| | |
|---|---|
| Vera and Linus decided to break into a house … | 1.32.1 |
| Vera and Linus found a blind girl upon a bench … | 1.53.1 |
| Vera and Linus found a little bird … | 1.40.1 |
| Vera and Linus found a long and large box … | 1.5.1 |
| Vera and Linus found a tiny door … | 2.42.1 |
| Vera and Linus had a wager. | 1.24.1 |
| Vera and Linus had a wager. The loser … | 1.45.1 |
| Vera and Linus had a wager where the winner … | 1.35.1 |
| Vera and Linus had marionettes cut … | 1.66.1 |
| Vera and Linus knew of a woman in the district … | 1.11.1 |
| Vera and Linus laid down a circle of conches … | 1.30.2 |
| Vera and Linus lay in bed … | 2.47.1 |
| Vera and Linus learned of a woman … | 2.8.1 |
| Vera and Linus looked out a little window … | 1.37.1 |
| Vera and Linus pretended that they were … | 1.43.1 |
| Vera and Linus retained possession … | 1.28.4 |
| Vera and Linus saw a girl … | 1.22.1 |
| Vera and Linus set out to construct … | 2.41.1 |
| Vera and Linus stood on the beach early … | 1.6.1 |
| Vera and Linus stood upon the cliffs … | 1.26.1 |
| Vera and Linus took a child … | 2.6.1 |
| Vera and Linus took themselves to a house … | 2.7.1 |
| Vera and Linus took themselves to a madhouse … | 2.30.1 |
| Vera and Linus took to the hills … | 2.20.1 |
| Vera and Linus undid the ropes … | 2.15.1 |
| Vera and Linus up to a mountain … | 1.50.1 |
| Vera and Linus wanted to procure … | 1.55.1 |
| Vera and Linus went about in a dense … | 2.29.2 |
| Vera and Linus went to bury the book … | 2.1.1 |
| Vera and Linus went to someone's countryhouse … | 2.46.1 |
| Vera and Linus went together to the house … | 2.12.1 |
| Vera and Linus went walking in the middle … | 2.49.1 |
| Vera and Linus were on a deserted … | 1.59.1 |
| Vera and Linus were vexed … | 1.30.1 |
| Vera and Linus were walking along a narrow … | 1.12.1 |

| | |
|---|---|
| Vera and Linus were walking along a promenade ... | 1.42.1 |
| Vera and Linus wondered whether a plant ... | 1.28.5 |
| Vera approached Linus ... | 1.65.1 |
| Vera assembled all the leaders ... | 2.35.1 |
| Vera began to hunt for a heart ... | 1.28.2 |
| Vera came home with a thing ... | 1.41.1 |
| Vera came to, motionless ... | 1.63.1 |
| Vera climbed up a high and graceful tree. | 1.15.1 |
| Vera decided to hide from Linus. | 1.2.1 |
| Vera decided to hide from Linus ... | 1.58.1 |
| Vera decided to set a riddle-path. | 2.45.3 |
| Vera drew a map of the death of honor ... | 2.45.2 |
| Vera dug a hole ... | 2.45.1 |
| Vera found a little box in the grass ... | 1.57.1 |
| Vera found a man who knew ... | 2.38.1 |
| Vera had never been to this place before ... | 1.10.1 |
| Vera painted wrinkles on herself ... | 1.49.1 |
| Vera, said Linus one day. Why not be ... | 2.39.1 |
| Vera sat in the kitchen ... | 1.28.6 |
| Vera stood by the open kitchen window ... | 1.8.1 |
| Vera summoned all who were still living ... | 2.31.1 |
| Vera thought it would be quite funny ... | 2.30.2 |
| Vera turned away from the little tea party. | 2.22.1 |
| Vera waited inside the room with the victim ... | 1.3.1 |
| Vera walked into a hallway where ... | 1.34.1 |
| Vera walked upon the street. | 1.28.1 |
| Vera was alone walking in the forest. | 1.14.1 |
| Vera was, as we know, a ... | 2.34.1 |
| Vera went into a crowd as you ... | 2.27.1 |
| Vera woke in a comfortable warmth ... | 2.21.1 |
| Vera woke in the afternoon. | 2.26.1 |
| Vera wrote a poem that could compel her. | 2.13.1 |
| With what book can you ... | 2.50.1 |